THE TROUBLE IN WARD J

Betty Carter was appointed assistant chief nurse of Ward J — known as the gremlin ward as things never went smoothly in it — and ordered to clear up the trouble there. The ward's chief nurse, Linda MacDonnell, resented Betty because she thought a professional nurse should refuse to think of romance or anything outside her profession — and Betty would not admit either that Ward J was jinxed or that to be a good nurse one had to forget that one was a woman.

Books by William Neubauer
in the Linford Romance Library:

ANGEL MOUNTAIN

WILLIAM NEUBAUER

THE TROUBLE IN WARD J

Complete and Unabridged

LINFORD
Leicester

First published in the
United States of America

First Linford Edition
published 1996

British Library CIP Data

Neubauer, William
   The trouble in Ward J.—Large print ed.—
Linford romance library
   1. American fiction—20th century
   2. Large type books
   I. Title
   813.5′4 [F]

   ISBN 0–7089–7972–6

Published by
F. A. Thorpe (Publishing) Ltd.
Anstey, Leicestershire

Set by Words & Graphics Ltd.
Anstey, Leicestershire
Printed and bound in Great Britain by
T. J. Press (Padstow) Ltd., Padstow, Cornwall

This book is printed on acid-free paper

1

THE forearm amputation went beautifully from the first anterior skin incision to the last interrupted suture over the through-and-through rubber drain. But it had been an arduous morning even for an energetic, thoroughly trained surgeon bidding for a Butterick Hospital residency. As the patient was guerneyed out, Dr. Lee Vaughan stripped off his gloves and cap-mask and ordered, "Wrap it up." Nor could Miss Ayres cajole him into doing the slated cholecystectomy before lunch. Much to scrub nurse Betty Ruth Carter's delight, Dr. Vaughan snapped to Miss Ayres, "I've had it." And that was that. He was gone long before the chief surgical nurse could switch from cajolery to appeal to higher authority. Miss Ayres frowned. She announced to Dr. Peake, "I doubt I'll adore that redhead." Then, like a sensible, unmarried woman of thirty, Miss Ayres chucklingly amended: "Unless, of course, he notices me."

Tired, trouble by stiffness between the shoulder blades, Betty Carter stepped down gingerly from the floor bench to lid the bucket containing the forearm. A very junior roust hustled over with an orange transfer ticket and a ballpoint pen. Most earnestly the girl said, "Dr. Boyd wants that thing yesterday, Miss Carter. Isn't his research project exciting?"

Betty made out the ticket and passed it to the chief surgeon for his signature. Dr. Peake scrawled. "You know, Miss Carter," he said expansively, "I think Vaughan's our man. I like a surgeon who bores in and gets the job done."

"Wonderful, sir."

He gave her a long glance. "How wonderful, Carter? Wonderful enough to make you bleat?"

The room went dead quiet.

Carefully, not looking at anyone,

Betty reminded him with a smile, "A Butterick graduate, sir, never bleats to her superiors. It just isn't done."

He gestured violently, as if to brush nonsense aside. "I don't care about good form, I don't care a hoot about it, Carter. I see a possibility of getting Surgery I on a sound footing. Vaughan and you would make the heart of a good team. That's all I'm interested in."

Miss Ayres came over quickly, not a supervisor afraid to defend her own. "Trot along," she told Betty. "That back must be killing you."

Miss Ayres took the orange ticket from Dr. Peake and gave it to the junior roust. "Medwick," she said, "research waits for no girl, so you run." Next, Miss Ayres swung around and got the clean-up crew working. But all the noise and the rather pointed hints failed. Dr. Peake stayed put near the head of the operating table, his piercing gray eyes challenging Betty to leave. Betty stayed put, too.

"I can't order you to bleat, Carter," Dr. Peake growled. "I do know, however, that I can bleat and that I will. You won't be transferred from my department if bleating will prevent it, believe me."

Casually, Miss Ayres took Betty by the arm. "Sir," she said, using more direct tactics, "Betty here can't be ordered to bleat for the simple reason that no one will listen if she does. It isn't a question of good form or what she's willing or not willing to do. A nurse just can't protest a transfer. And I meant *can't*; not *may not*. There just aren't channels through which bleats can be routed."

"Preposterous!"

Quietly, skillfully, Miss Ayres began a general drift toward the autoclave-room doorway. The maneuver was noticed. For a moment, just for a moment, Betty was positive there'd be a scene. She heard Dr. Peake draw a sharp and whistling breath. She heard one of the students giggle nervously. But the maneuver paid off. It was either begin a scene or let them leave, and Dr. Peake held his tongue. They reached the door, they were through the door, and a scurry got them to the sanctuary of the nurses' dressing room. Eyes dancing like a happy teen-ager's, Miss Ayres closed and locked the door behind them. "The things I must do for you idiots," she deplored. "Why are all women under thirty complete idiots?"

"Thanks, Mary."

"Quite all right. You realize, of course, that it was your fault? During that forearm amputation, you came in with a hold on the muslin retractor just in time to spare Dr. Vaughan inconvenience. Naturally, Dr. Peake noticed. Naturally, Dr. Peake did a slow burn from that second on."

"Dr. Vaughan was playing out."

"Oh, I don't know."

"I do. Just before the bone saw came through the ulna, Dr. Vaughan's tempo slowed at least ten counts a minute."

"Really?"

Betty hampered her gown. Methodically, she thrust her arms straight out sideways and rotated them slowly, in clockwise fashion, to work the kinks from her back. It surprised her when Miss Ayres took a straight-backed chair near the uniform drum. "Those cleanup people need supervision," she warned. "Ann's getting them trained, but they need more time."

"Possibly this is more important."

Miss Ayres' voice, a combination of exasperation and brusqueness, suggested not too subtly that they were supervisor and subordinate again. Betty grinned affectionately, thinking that she'd miss this woman who never appeared quite comfortable in the oddball position she occupied between the old guard and the comers.

"The fact is," Mary Ayres said, "that Dr. Peake's argument is reasonable. He has three surgeries up here to supervise, and the one down in emergency, to boot. Surgery 1 has been a clunker, let's face it. Dr. Benson was good but slow, and Dr. Carstairs was less good and slow. Now Vaughan has come up from the ranks, and Vaughan's good and Vaughan's fast. All right. Now Dr. Peake has a chance to serve this city with three top flight surgeries. Why wouldn't it tee him off to lose a good scrub just when he's getting Surgery 1 squared away?"

Betty said pleasantly but firmly, "I won't protest the transfer, Miss Ayres. I won't ask for any special consideration, either. I've come this far in Butterick with a clean record, and I won't spoil it now by bleating."

"In other words, Dr. Vincent Wynkoop is prettier?"

Betty dropped her hands to her sides. She took off her hospital-issue underclothes and hampered them, too. A slender brunette, she set off jauntily for the shower.

Miss Ayres stopped her in her tracks by asking, "Why on earth, I wonder, are you so positive you'll end up in the rehab center under Dr. Wynkoop?

Everyone knows the not-so-pretty chase you're leading Dr. Wynkoop and Dr. Huebner. The personnel office isn't staffed by idiots. They're all thirty or older down there."

"He's asked for me, you see." But, worried, Betty put on a terry-cloth robe and took the chair next to Miss Ayres. "What have you heard, Miss Ayres?"

Miss Ayres began to hum, clearly enjoying the effect of her question.

A horrible thought occurred to Betty Ruth Carter. "Not Ward J," she all but moaned. "Glory, not Ward J!"

Little Miss Ayres took her hand and patted it and waxed implausibly maternal. "You said that, dear, not I. But certainly you have to admit it's a possibility. Do you admit that?"

"If it happens, I'll bleat!"

"Ah, but by then it won't do any good. By then your replacement will be assigned to us, and you couldn't come back here even if Mrs. Dolezal wanted you to. See how feminine common sense and logic sweep all things before

8

it? Now here's what you do. You bleat now. If you win, we win. But if you lose, you don't lose everything. I'm sure the personnel office wouldn't ignore your wishes twice in a row. They're not monsters down there."

The telephone interrupted.

Dr. Vincent Wynkoop's office, Ludmilla speaking. "Miss Carter," Ludmilla asked, "when are you due to report in personnel?"

"High noon."

"I see. Well, something's come up, Miss Carter. There isn't time to brief you completely now, but for some reasons he'll explain later, Dr. Wynkoop called back that bid for your services here."

"What?"

"Now you're not to fret, Miss Carter. Miss Haskell knows Dr. Wynkoop's wishes, and he's sure she'll do her best for him. But there's a lot of political hatchet work going on right now, and Dr. Wynkoop thinks it wise to handle it this way."

"Let me talk to Vince, please."

"Oh, that would be impossible just now, Miss Carter. Dr. Peake came over just a minute or so ago, and they've gone out to lunch."

Softly, her mind racing, Betty returned the handset to the wall hook. Miss Ayres, her face and manner bland, asked concernedly, "No bad news, I hope. Why, you've lost color!"

Betty asked furiously, "All right, Mary, what gives? Vince has pulled back his bid and is lunching right now with Dr. Peake."

"Why would I know what's going on?"

"I have news for you, Mary. It so happens that I've dreamed for more than a year of working over in rehab. I happen to love the idea of helping handicapped people adapt to their new physical condition. Sure, Vince dates me, as Rolfe dates me, and maybe we've kissed a few times. But Vince has nothing to do with my interest in rehab nursing. So if I'm chopped

10

off there, you and Dr. Peake will be sorry."

"Whoa. Never threaten an immediate supervisor or department head."

Betty rushed to her locker and took her clothes out and started to dress. For two or three minutes Miss Ayres just stood there watching, a cool smile on her face. Something in Betty's manner, though, suddenly made Miss Ayres uneasy. She said abruptly, "I happen to be fond of you, Betty. Candidly, you're one of the most amiable scrubs I've ever had. But when I'm on the job, I'm paid to do the job to the very best of my ability. I owe it to my job to keep you here if I can."

Pain lanced through Betty's back as she tried to hook her bra. Clucking, Miss Ayres came over and did the hooking for her. "I'll make a deal," Miss Ayres proposed. "Bleat to Haskell, like a good girl, and I'll get you weekends off."

Betty got her uniform on, and Miss Ayres saw to the snaps and buttons.

Presently Miss Mary Ayres sighed. "All right, all right," she said. "Dr. Wynkoop wants some special equipment over in rehab. He needs one more vote at the department-head meeting tomorrow. I imagine the men have made a deal."

"For shame!"

"I won't apologize."

Betty pinned on her cap.

"Now if you bleat," Miss Ayres said, "I think you'll come back to loving me for another year."

Made queasy by disappointment, Betty got out of there before she really lost her temper. She went straight to the personnel office in the sub-basement. Miss Haskell's secretary studied her face amusedly. "Why do all you nurses have transfer blues?" she asked. "Secretaries around here should have it so good!" She glanced at her desk clock. "Better early than late," she commented, and led Betty along a short hall to Miss Haskell's office. "Miss Carter, Miss Haskell," she said. She put a chair beside the desk and left. Betty was motioned to take the chair. "Not that we'll be long," Miss Haskell said, "but I understand you've done four majors this morning."

"Yes, ma'am."

"Well, take the afternoon off. I'll arrange it with surgery I. Now as to your next assignment: frankly, we've not decided. I know that Dr. Peake wants to keep you and that Dr. Wynkoop would like to have you. Also, I know you've stated a preference for rehab nursing. But an interesting thing's happened, Miss Carter. Ever since your name was circulated on the transfer list, I've received bids for your services. I realize there's a nursing shortage, but that can't account for your popularity. Other girls are passed over. Can it be that you're competent?"

Dutifully, Betty smiled.

"Well, pop in at eight tomorrow, Miss Carter. I imagine Mrs. Dolezal will have her recommendation in by then."

Betty opened her mouth to protest. Miss Haskell's face hardened. Seething, Betty nodded and left.

2

APOUTING, sleepy-eyed Ann Osgood was having coffee on the cottage porch when Betty got home. On the porch rail farthest from Ann sat a small gray squirrel that was obviously waiting for decent privacy in which to invade the bird-feeder platform. Ann was trying to lure the squirrel to her hand with peanut butter and crackers. The squirrel was interested, but not rashly so. Ann's pout could be clearly traced to the squirrel's unwillingness to trust her. Ann hated not being trusted by anything that wiggled, crawled or flew. It was a matter of pride to Ann that even scared children quieted down the instant she stepped into an anesthesia room to comfort them. That mean old squirrel!

Moving quite slowly to avoid

frightening the beast, Betty mounted the porch and took the wicker chair nearest the coffeepot. "Feel better?" she asked. "You could've stayed in bed until Rolfe examined you."

"Do you like squirrels?"

"Well, that depends. I've eaten good squirrel pie and poor squirrel pie. If you use the proper herbs, I like squirrel."

"Very unfunny."

Betty chirped to the squirrel. The squirrel leaned forward. Betty took a cracker and spread some peanut butter on it. She got up and walked easily toward the squirrel, holding the chow out and chirping softly. The squirrel reared back on its haunches and actually thrust its forepaws out for the chow. Betty gave it the cracker and went back to her chair.

Ann said flatly, "You didn't do that. I never saw you do that."

"The trouble with you, Ann, is that you weren't raised on a farm. To get anywhere with animals, be gentle but be direct."

Her eyes sparkling excitedly, Ann rose slowly and inched her way toward the squirrel. But this was a mean old squirrel, all right. The squirrel streaked toward Betty's chair by way of the railing. Betty spread peanut butter on another cracker and set the cracker on her left knee. The squirrel jumped to her lap and arranged itself comfortably to dine. Ann Osgood said not a word. Ann leaned back against the building and brooded.

"I've always been able to handle wild creatures," Betty told her. "When I was knee-high to a squealer pig, I had quite a menagerie: two raccoons, two possums, a skunk, several king snakes, a regular herd of sun lizards. No cages, you understand. My folks don't believe in cages, nor do I."

"On a *farm*?"

"Oh, you're wondering about the chickens and such. Dad just made the coops more or less impregnable. The point I'm making, though, is that you either have a way with animals or you don't. Or put it this way: you either have a way with scared children or you don't. I can never quiet the little darlings in an anesthesia room."

"And being a farm girl, I suppose you'll now fatten that poor dear for your table."

"Naturally."

"Betty Ruth Carter, you wouldn't!"

Betty scratched the squirrel's left ear. "Don't you ever try this with a wild squirrel," she ordered. "A wild animal really shouldn't ever be touched."

"Whatever you can do, I can do. Except pass instruments, of course. How did Dr. Vaughan do? I really hated not being there. There's pressure enough on a candidate without the added pressure of Miss Ayres' attendance as chief roust."

"He did quite well. He tailed off toward the end in various little ways, but even the forearm amputation went beautifully. He's it, Ann. Dr. Peake practically said as much."

"What about you? It would be quite a team, wouldn't it? We're all about the same age, and we're all interested in surgery."

"I didn't bleat and I won't bleat. To be honest, I've been looking forward to this transfer for a long time. I want rehab work. And if you dare to hint or even think that Dr. Wynkoop is the reason, I'll serve you this squirrel for breakfast."

"Betty, he's snoozing! Will you look at that darling? He's snoozing!"

"Naturally. All guys are alike. Fill their bellies, and they'll doze off every time."

"Ah, let me hold him. Will you please let me hold him?"

"It wouldn't be wise, Ann. Truly. Let's tame him first. In a few days he'll be lolling all over you, just wait and see."

A sound startled the squirrel. He leaped to the railing with a prodigious push of his hind legs. Betty felt the needle-like claws through her skirt and had to laugh. "Powerful little fellow," she commented.

A car came into sight on the earthen road between the two-story frame farmhouse and the ecucalyptus-tree windbreak. The car came on steadily to the low white picket fence of the cottage property. Ann stopped, peered and blinked. "Lawsy me, master," she said, "it's Linda 'Hot Shot' MacDonnell in person."

"Nonsense."

But it was Linda, all right, as beautiful and poised as ever, her blue-black hair glossy in the sunshine, her big violet eyes looking amused by their surprise. "A truce," Linda begged, mounting the stoop. "My, what a lovely rental!"

Ann got stiffly to her knees and made a fair imitation of a salaam.

"Be sweet," Linda urged. "Be your natural self, Osgood."

"Is that an order, O Wheel?"

"Whoa," Betty told Ann. "She's on our territory and out of uniform."

20

Linda smiled faintly. She selected a chair that gave her a grand view of the Hardin City River purling south. "How'd you find this place?" she asked Betty. "I must've scoured this town for a suitable place, and I didn't ever see one that could compare with this."

"Actually, Rolfe found it, Linda. He went out with the emergency crew one day. Mrs. Morden, who lives in that farmhouse, was painting the bathroom while all the windows and doors were closed. She was overcome by the fumes, and Mr. Morden called Butterick. It was a no-sweat duty, really. Mrs. Morden had revived by the time the ambulance arrived. Anyway, Rolfe got to talking with the Mordens, and they mentioned that they have this cottage available. We looked, we liked, we rented. I think we're in on a good deal, because the Mordens like having nurses around at all hours."

"How many rooms?"

"Two bedrooms," Ann said. "And if you're thinking what I think you're thinking, knock it off. I do *not* adore my former classmate Linda MacDonnell. I think what my former classmate did to Reta Olney was a despicable thing to do to any human being. Have I made myself clear?"

"Now, now," Linda said easily, "just be your natural sweet self. Mrs. Dolezal conducted a hearing, and she upheld the discharge. Everyone did, in fact."

"Just the same, I've said it and I'm glad."

Huffily, Ann went indoors and made considerable noise locking and then bolting the front door.

Linda stirred disgustedly. "Girl to girl," she said, "I think Ann ought to grow up emotionally. Really! She doesn't help herself when she says things like that. I don't think Butterick has ever had a better chief roust nurse, and she could go far. I have an idea that right now she hasn't any real competition for that job on Miss Ayres' staff."

"Ann was fond of Reta," Betty

explained. "They were roomies in student days."

"Still — "

"I was quite surprised to see you," Betty said, bluntly changing the subject. "I'm afraid you've come at a poor time, though. I'm up for transfer, and they're playing it cool."

"I thought they'd never pull you out of Surgery 1."

"Apparently Dr. Peake thought so, too. It jarred him when he found my name on that transfer list they circulate once a month. By then, of course, it was too late for him to do very much through channels."

Linda was quick, almost frighteningly quick. "What has he done outside of channels," she asked, "to put that nasty little gleam in your eyes?"

"Hang it, he's making it very difficult for me to land a slot at the rehab center!"

"Oh?"

"I sometimes think," Betty said gloomily, "that I ought to call it a career and marry either Rolfe Huebner or Vince Wynkoop."

"Marriage solves nothing. As a matter of fact, marriage complicates what can be a good life."

"Care to give a former classmate a tip on how to land the job she wants?"

Linda just looked.

"Question withdrawn," Betty said lightly. "Now then, Linda, what can I do for you?"

"You haven't changed much, Betty, have you? You ought to have learned the value of subtlety by this time. Well, no matter. Miss Haskell telephoned a suggestion I ought to come chat with you and look you over. Ward 1 needs an R.N., and you're due for a transfer. Think you could work under the supervision of a former classmate?"

"No."

Linda chuckled. "It's dreadful to be as unpopular as I, Betty. Some pay days I weep as I carry my chief nurse pay check to the bank."

"And I'll tell you more," Betty said flatly. "If I must accept Ward J or resign, then I'll resign."

If Linda felt offended, she never betrayed the emotion. "At least you're blunt about it," she murmured.

"I insist I'm not as wicked as I'm reputed to be, however. All of you self-appointed judges overlook an important fact. The fact is that you're not qualified to judge. None of you has made chief nurse rank. None of you has responsibility for a huge ward. You haven't the vaguest notion what a chief nurse must do and why she must do it. Take Ann, ready to claw me because I lowered the boom on Reta Olney. Would you care to know why I lowered the boom?"

"It isn't pertinent, as the lawyers say."

"But it is, Betty, it is. I lowered the boom because Reta goofed off. Too many patients weren't being given the attention they were entitled to. I have an old-fashioned notion that a charity case deserves just as much attention as a billionaire. I insisted on a professional attitude and on professional work at all times. But Reta goofed off and goofed off. One fine day there was a complication with an amputee because Reta neglected to check the stump dressing. That was when I discharged her."

Betty stared.

Linda shrugged. "Now why did I tell you this, Betty? Simple. Too many know-nothing people call Ward J a jinx ward or a gremlin ward because so many things seem to go wrong there. The fact is that things go quite well there, for a ward so large, if the nurses and their crews do the job they've been trained to do and are paid to do."

"Just the same, Linda — "

Briefly, Linda lost her iron control. "Oh, stop being blind and stupid, Carter! It should have occurred to you before this that I'm here because you've been transferred to me. Why else would I visit you?"

Betty swallowed. For at least a full minute that was all she could do, over and over and over again, like a dumfounded child. Finally she managed to murmur, "I see."

"I'm not any happier about it than you, Carter. I picked someone else from the transfer list, but Miss Haskell gave me you. You're too free and easy in your general approach to professional discipline. I know you do top work, but I need more than that in Ward 1."

"Well, relax, Linda I'll resign, and you'll probably get your choice."

Linda's lips tightened. Betty got the idea, then, that Linda had really come to sell the job to her. She felt guilty as Linda got up and headed for her car. Still, Betty managed to sit there wooden-faced until Linda had driven away.

3

IT was after eleven o'clock the next morning when Betty Carter, dressed in a brown tweed suit but hatless, entered Miss Haskell's private office in the personnel department of Butterick Hospital. Miss Haskell looked up at her coolly and motioned for her to be seated. "I received your special delivery letter about an hour ago," Miss Haskell reported. "It surprised me. According to all the information I have on you in the files, you have all the desirable qualifications for an operating room nurse. You're physically strong, you have patience and forbearance, you're cool under pressure, you're alert, you have self-control. Most of all, you have the ability to think. So the records tell me. But after I'd read that letter, Miss Carter . . . well, let me simply say I'd have expected better from even a probationer."

Betty, her cheeks burning, managed to hold her tongue.

"I humor everyone," Miss Haskell said, "even foolish children. A transcript of your record here is being made. I imagine we'll need another half-hour or so."

"May I wait?"

"Certainly. Keep Dr. Wynkoop and Dr. Huebner out of this, though, will you? By that I mean, please don't badger either of them into doing something rash. Men can be badgered, I understand."

"I thought I'd just wait in your reception room, Miss Haskell."

"Oh, I see. You have a position lined up, then?"

"I believe so. My mother still has medical connections in Hardin City. I telephoned her in Oregon. She telephoned Dr. Oglethorpe, Dr. Oglethorpe telephoned me. I'm to be his office nurse, if I wish. I dare say I'll be his scrub, too, whenever he undertakes a surgery."

Miss Haskell's brows came together over her faintly snubbed nose. "You're quite serious, then, I take it."

"I deserved better."

"In what way?"

"Miss Haskell, the record shows I've never been a bleater or a sulker. From the day I entered training here I obeyed every rule, I did every job assigned me. And I studied well enough and I worked well enough to win commendations from teachers and supervisors and department heads. All right. No one has the right to say where she'll work here. I know that as well as you. But a girl does have the right, I think, to resent shabby treatment. I've done nothing, absolutely nothing, to deserve banishment to Ward J. So rather than take it and rather than bleat, I quit."

"Simmer down, Miss Carter."

Betty started for the door.

With something like laughter in her voice, Miss Haskell asked, "Why do you assume, Miss Carter, that a person of my experience would know less about your record here than you do? Studying records is my specialty."

"Then — "

"Let me show you something, please."

Betty hesitated at the door. Reluctantly, she went back to the desk. Miss Haskell handed her a transfer slip and said, "The thing I want you to notice is the title that follows your name. Assistant chief nurse. I didn't know that even in these strange times, workers considered promotions to be punishments or banishments."

Betty sat on the armchair. She had to.

"Now let's be entirely practical," Miss Haskell said briskly. "We can't afford to lose you in this period of nurse shortage, and you can't afford to refuse a promotion that carries with it more money, professional prestige and opportunity. Take opportunity for a moment. Up in the surgical department, you have a brilliant Miss Ayres who's good for about thirty years more of service as chief surgical nurse. Regardless of how brilliantly you performed, you couldn't get ahead up there. In the wards, the situation is different. You see that in Miss MacDonnell's case. At twenty-six she heads a ward. At twenty-six, or a year from now, you could head a ward. It's that simple."

"I'd rather do rehab nursing. If I can't have that, give me bedside nursing. Give me recovery room duty."

"Be sensible, please."

"Miss Haskell, I didn't become a nurse to become an administrator."

"Well, we can argue about that next year. The point is that your record shows little ward experience. So ward duty is indicated, and ward duty it is unless you really do quit."

"Then some other ward. Any ward but Ward J."

"Sorry. The promotion indicates our opinion of you, our hope of keeping you, of moving you ahead. You go talk that over with Dr. Huebner, if you wish. I think he'll tell you the need in Ward J is rather serious and that no one here in the hospital just pulled your name out of a hat."

"What on earth has Rolfe to do with it, Miss Haskell?"

"Simple. The resident in medicine gets around from ward to ward. While his first concern is for the patients, he naturally sees many things as he makes his rounds. He's seen you in action in various jobs. So when he saw the list of nurses we'd drawn up for consideration for the Ward J appointment, he stated in writing that he would choose you."

Betty gritted her teeth.

"Interestingly," Miss Haskell continued, "even Dr. Vincent Wynkoop thought you'd be best for that job. Of course, he still bid for you, but he did write you were the best of the lot on that list."

Betty thought dourly that she'd turn both fellows in for a new model the first chance she got.

"It's Ward J or you're out," Miss Haskell said flatly. "And let me tell you this, Miss Carter. Had your record as a student and a nurse at Butterick not been excellent, you'd be out right now. As it is, you have an hour in which to reconsider this preposterous letter of resignation."

Miss Haskell held the letter out. Betty took it, feeling oddly on the defensive, and got out of the office before Miss Haskell could spring any more surprises on her. Automatically she went up to Rolfe's cubbyhole office on the third floor. He was at his desk, still in a white smock, looking through a batch of ward notes. He grinned approval of the attractive appearance she made in the tweed suit. "I must marry you one of these years," he said. "Remind me."

"Heavy workload?"

"The usual."

"It's rather early for lunch, but I'll buy."

"A rich nurse and her money are soon parted. I was told that back in medical school by a professor who understood I was having financial difficulties. He offered to introduce me to some rich nurses at the hospital the school operated in conjunction with the city."

"And did you separate any rich nurses from their money?"

"Well, I'm a doctor, it seems. What do you think?"

He looked so pleased with the retort that Betty just had to go around the desk and kiss the tip of his ear. "I never get enough of that," he said. "I'm afraid I'll end up marrying you sooner or later. Now what's the problem?"

"You know darned well what the problem is."

"Ward J?"

"Ward J."

He switched off the desk lamp, chuckling. "I heard about it from Vince Wynkoop. I suppose Dr. Peake's trying to wiggle out of that deal he made with Vince to keep your services."

"Don't doctors have anything to do around here but concern themselves with the nurses?"

"Well," he said as to a child, "the nurses around here happen to be women, and we happen to be men."

When he was in the mood for such nonsense, Betty knew, she could never get the better of him. And that struck her, now as always, as strange. Rolfe Huebner was the overly serious, dedicated type of doctor few would ever associate with nonsense. Unless some maternal soul kept an eye on him, he'd work with quiet energy at his job at least sixteen hours a day, seldom stopping to rest or even to eat. But for some fantastic reason she brought out the mischief in him that few suspected lay covered up by his professional manner. And once that sense of mischief had been brought out — *pow*!

"What do I do?" she asked plaintively. "Rolfe, I blew my stack yesterday afternoon. Linda came out and put it on about my lack of subtlety and conveyed without ever saying so that it would be gracious of her to accept me in Ward J."

"And you quarreled?"

"Well, not exactly." Betty moved some of the papers from the corner of the desk. She let part of herself down onto the cleared space but kept much of her weight on her right leg. "I dare say you'd call it a typically nasty-nice quarrel. We weren't adoring one another, I'll concede that. Anyway, she finally made a few criticisms of my judgment and professional approach, and I told her to relax, because I'd resign rather than work under her."

"But you weren't spatting. Goodness me no, you weren't spatting!"

Betty's brown eyes flashed. "Well, by the time her car disappeared, I was angry enough to blow battleships out of the water. In the end I wrote a hot letter of resignation and put it in the mail, special delivery. Miss Haskell got it first thing this morning."

Rolfe wagged his head.

"I won't crawl to Linda, I'll tell you

that, Rolfe. There's something about that girl that always did raise the fuzz on my nape. We were deadly rivals during our student days. Candidly, I was a poorer student than my grades will ever show. My pride wouldn't allow me to let Linda swamp me as she was swamping all our other classmates."

"Do you know what, Betty?"

"What?"

"You've been spoiled."

"Thank you, good sir. Don't invite yourself over for the usual Saturday evening dinner. I'll call you."

Rolfe regarded her thoughtfully. "But you've been spoiled just the same," he insisted. "It figures, of course. You're attractive, you have personality, you work hard, you're amiable. Supervisors find you a joy to have around, so they spoil you outrageously to keep you around. But look here. Just for the record I'd like to remind you this is a hospital; not a battleground created by man and God for warfare between Linda MacDonnell and Betty Ruth Carter. People are ill or in pain or dying or getting well in our wards, remember. They need nursing care, among other things. We exist to give them all they need, and you're here to see to some of the nursing."

"I'll take anything but Ward J. I told Miss Haskell that."

"So, naturally, she told you it would be Ward J or else."

Betty eyed him suspiciously. "Did she telephone you a few minutes ago?"

"No. Her ultimatum figures, that's all. If she yielded to pressure tactics just once, the transfer system we use here would be washed up. It's a good system. If I were at her desk, I'd keep the system if I had to lose a good nurse in the process."

"Darn it, couldn't you talk to her unofficially?"

"No."

"Meaning you won't?"

"Right."

"Oh, and about our usual Saturday

night dinner: don't hang around waiting for me to call this Saturday."

Rolfe turned back to the ward reports. "Did it ever occur to you," he asked, "that Linda MacDonnell might be on her way out?"

"What? But that's ridiculous! Glory knows I don't like her, but she's a positively brilliant nurse."

"Ward J is a mess," Rolfe said harshly. "Something's happening there to give Mrs. Dolezal and the powers that be serious headaches. Frankly, I think the fault is Linda's."

"Rolfe, that's unfair! Do you feel well?"

"If you don't take the assignment, Betty, someone else will — maybe one of these efficient, deadly, ruthless, ambitious girls we're developing these days. What a spot for such a girl! A second in command writes ward reports, too, you know. A clever girl could do some effective back-stabbing in her reports if things continued to go badly in Ward J."

"Rolfe, you're talking about nurses; not about women with a chance to make a fortune if they stab the front-runners in the back."

"I checked your name on the list, Betty, because I knew you'd do a fair and conscientious job if you took the job. Now get out of here. I'm busy. And about the usual Saturday dinner you won't cook me this week: it doesn't matter. Have you ever met Baby Doll Langdahl?"

"Who?"

"She sings in one of the local night clubs. She popped in the other evening, complaining of nausea and the like. I found out she was auditioning for a local television show and gave her something to soothe her nervous stomach. She got the job on the show. Grateful, as all beautiful redheads ought to be, she invited me to have dinner at her apartment this Saturday evening. Do you think I should wear a necktie?"

Betty, to her astonishment, felt hotly

jealous. "Darn it," she snapped, "I hate men and I hate entertainers!"

But, of course, she took Rolfe's thinly veiled advice and went back to Miss Haskell and apologized and fibbed, "I'd just *love* to be assigned to Ward J, ma'am."

4

DR. ROLFE HUEBNER came anyway on Saturday, arriving in mid-afternoon with a peace offering in the form of a bottle of Wente Brothers Gray Reisling wine. He solicitously inquired about the state of Ann Osgood's health. "Little fish like you," he told her, "ought to know better than to try to shift boulders around. It's astonishing you didn't do more than strain your shoulders."

Ann glanced at Betty. Her thin dimpled face showing no expression whasoever, Ann asked, "Did you want to reach the Happy Hour before or after Baby Doll Langdahl has done her evening show?"

"Rolfe," Betty asked, "is she worth hearing? You have to pay a Federal tax, you know, if you're there while the entertainment is on."

"Lovely afternoon, isn't it?" Rolfe asked. "I admire yonder shrubs. What are they?"

"Bridal wreath. I'm not hinting, you understand; just answering your question."

Chuckling, Rolfe removed his jacket and went up to the porch. "That wine should be well chilled," he commented. "It ought to go well with the fish cakes."

"I plan to wear that dreamy lime-green dress to the Happy Hour," Ann told Betty. "I suppose I should've gotten my rubies and diamonds out of the safe-deposit box, but I forgot. I don't think it matters, though. How could any girl distract attention from Baby Doll?"

"Just keep right on," Rolfe threatened, "and someone gets a pop on the chin."

Betty took the wine to the refrigerator. She went to check the condition of her bedroom, and then went on to make certain the guest towels were on the bar in the bathroom. While she was going back to the porch, the telephone rang in the living room. It was Linda MacDonnell, her voice a lovely contralto as it came over the wire.

"I understand," Linda said, "that you've accepted duty in Ward J."

"Hi, Linda."

"Miss MacDonnell, Betty. It's never well, I think, for supervisor and subordinate to be buddy-buddy."

"What about coming in Monday morning at seven? That'll give me an hour to familiarize you with the ward and our way of doing things."

"Of course, Miss MacDonnell."

Ann and Rolfe came in. Rolfe had his shirt off now. It was quite evident that he'd come for a good afternoon of gardening and that he was anxious to get going.

"I hope you understand," Linda said, "that I'm not interested in stressing rank. The regulations require a certain formality, that's all."

"I understand, Miss MacDonnell."

"Good. You might give thought this weekend to the shift you want. I plan to use you in two capacities: as my administrative assistant and as the head of one of the shifts. You may choose four-to-midnight or midnight-to-eight."

"What?"

"Midnight-to-eight is when we have the most difficulty, so I'd prefer to have you head that one. But I like to rule with an easy hand, so if you select four-to-midnight I'll indulge you."

"But my social life!"

"Now, now, now," Linda said. "You know and I know that where there's a will, there's a way. I'm sure the fellows will find you regardless of your work hours."

"I protest!"

"Goodness, not officially, I hope."

Betty sighed, "No, ma'am," she said. "Never officially. I'd consider it a privilege to head the midnight-to-eight shift in Ward J."

There was a moment's silence.

"Well," Linda said in less brusque

tones, "come in at seven on Monday and we'll talk things over."

By the time Betty had hung up, Rolfe was putting on his work clothes in her bedroom. Ann took advantage of his absence to ask: "Graveyard?"

"Yup."

"It's interesting, isn't it, how predictable Linda's behavior is? I doubted, however, that she'd pull a thing like that so quickly."

"She's covered nicely, Ann. She told me the graveyard's the shift they have the most difficulty with. Its logical to put your second in command in the toughest slot. I'd do the same, you know. So would you."

"It'll certainly change our way of life. I'll be out while you're in, and vice versa."

"I'm afraid so."

Ann said a bit sheepishly, "I don't know if I'd have the nerve to be alone at night. It's inside the city limits, I know, but it can be awfully dark and quiet out here."

"Well, the Mordens aren't too far away."

Rolfe clamped in, wearing a sweatshirt, levi trousers and rubber-soled work shoes. "I thought I'd finish that rustic bridge," he announced. "I still think, though, that a Japanese-style bridge would've been prettier."

He noticed their glum faces. He folded his arms across his chest and said gently, "All right, girls, tell the family medic. You have the pip. Is that it? You've gone and caught the pip."

"Linda's stuck Betty with the graveyard shift, Rolfe. I think that's mean."

"Oh?"

"Ann," Betty said, "it isn't mean if the situation is as she's described it."

"Well, I don't think I could stay here alone at night for a minute. I'm not the brave type. I'd hear every sound for miles around, and if I slept at all, I'd do it with my head under the covers."

"Get another roomie, then," Rolfe

suggested. "It would lower your individual costs."

Ann's hazel eyes came alive. "Well, we *could* do that, of course. But who'd we take? You can't live with just anybody, you know."

Betty went restlessly toward the hall. "Well, you figure it out while Rolfe and I build that pesky bridge. In a pinch, there's always Ludmilla."

"She's so hearty!"

Chuckling, Betty led Rolfe outdoors. They went to the garage for the tools Mr. Morden had loaned them, and while they were carrying everything down to the river, old Mr. Morden came ambling along to watch and supervise. He pumped Rolfe's hand several times. "Doc," he said, "I like to see folks get outdoor exercise. Like I was telling Mrs. Morden, most docs never look healthy on account of they're indoors so much."

The project this afternoon was to check for accuracy all the pieces that had been cut, and then to get

49

the actualy construction under way. With a small tape measure, Betty checked each of the floor boards and then the posts and railings of the proposed bridge. Rolfe and Mr. Morden checked the lengths of the redwood boards that would support the whole structure. One board was found to be approximately two inches too long, so Rolfe had to get the handsaw and square and shorten it. Mr. Morden sat in the shade of a tan oak and watched, an angular man who had high cheekbones, a prominent jaw and a firm, rather carp-like mouth. After Rolfe had succeeded in making a reasonably square cut, Mr. Morden asked abruptly, "Miss Carter, why don't you buy this place? You love it enough to own it, and what you're doing right now as a renter just isn't very smart. What I mean is, you're improving the property with your own labor and your own money, and I could kick you out any time I wanted."

Betty laughed. "Absolutely, Mr. Morden! Do I give you my check for a million dollars here and now, or will you wait until later?"

"Say I said the cottage property's for sale. What would you offer?"

"I wouldn't offer what it's worth, Mr. Morden. All I have is my salary. I suppose I could write my rich parents in Oregon and borrow enough for the down payment, but the monthly payments would have to be low."

Mr. Morden shifted his gaze to Rolfe. "Doc," he asked, "would you say ten thousand's a fair price?"

"Two thousand. Now let's haggle from there."

"It sure beats me," Mr. Morden said, "how a man smart enough to fix up a person's insides can't learn even a little bit about business. Well, let me ask this."

"Are you and Miss Carter gonna be hitched?"

Betty sat down and whooped joyous laughter. "Talk about a shotgun wedding! Rolfe, kindly marry me this afternoon so we can make a clever buy here, will you?"

"Aw, I'd rather build a bridge."

Mr. Morden wagged his grizzled head. "Folks nowadays," he opined, "aren't as serious as they should be. Look, Miss Carter. Mrs. Morden and I feel sort of like we're cheating a nice girl by taking seventy-five a month from her just to let her live here. It just doesn't seem right. Now here's what I thought we'd do. You can have this place for nine thousand; not a cent less. I'll take two thousand for a down payment and carry a mortgage on the rest at six percent interest. That way, your rent money pays off the place; and even if you wanted to call it quits in a few years, you'd have an equity here and at least get your rent back. And what with Miss Osgood paying half, you'd be making a profit if you sold out just for equity. See?"

Betty drew a deep breath. The mere

thought of owning the lovely property thrilled her, but she knew so little about business she didn't know what to answer.

Rolfe said quietly, "I have a few thousand stashed away, Betty. If you want to borrow that, you're welcome. You know the great plan. Two years more as resident; then general practice. If I got the money back by then, it would be soon enough."

"Why I asked about the wedding," Mr. Morden said, "is that Mrs. Morden and I feel we owe you a debt, Dr. Huebner. We'd knock off fifteen hundred as a wedding gift."

A mauve-colored roadster came along the drive, its set of horns blaring a fine musical chord. The stunning redhead at the wheel noticed them, stopped the car and got out and came toward them, a fetching specimen of female pulchritude in a white playsuit that clung snugly to her figure. Rolfe put his tools down and said, "My, my, my." He went to meet the stunning woman, his smile broad, his movements quick and vigorous. "Nice surprise, Baby Doll," he called. "Have you ever seen a bridge built? You do this and that, and you have it made."

Her eyes, practically electric green, glowed first for him alone and then for any other animate creature within miles around. "I thought you'd like to see the television show," she explained. "I belt out the most romantic song you'll ever hear."

Rolfe made the introductions.

Baby Doll smiled sweetly at Betty. "Oh, you're that nurse," she said, "that gives Rolfe fits. How can you stand fiddling around in an operating room with someone's squishy insides?"

"Well, Baby Doll, that's a long story. It began in high-school biology, with a frog I was dissecting. But I'm sure you don't care to hear about that. Stay for dinner? Any girl of Rolfe's is a friend of mine."

For once, just for once, Betty had the satisfaction of seeing Rolfe stand there too dumbfounded to make with a witticism. Hugely pleased, she looked at Mr. Morden and winked.

5

GIVEN a week to think things over, Betty put the business deal out of her mind temporarily to concentrate upon professional matters. It was just as well she decided to do this, for on Sunday morning the doorbell was rung and she found the superintendent of nurses of Butterick Hospital standing on the porch. A tall, slender, dark-haired woman possessed of the most perfect poker face Betty had ever seen, Mrs. Dolezal further startled her by saying, "Good morning, Betty. Are you entirely alone? Ann's supposed to be on duty, but one never knows."

"She went off to work aching but game, Mrs. Dolezal. What a lovely surprise! Won't you come in? I was just having coffee."

"Our people drink too much coffee,

it seems to me." But Mrs. Dolezal did take a seat at the dinette and she did accept a cup of coffee. She glanced about inquisitively. "You do well here," she commented. "A home apparently means a great deal to you. I'm glad to know that. There's infinitely more to life than a professional grind."

"I'm the home and kiddies type, I dare say. Even as a tot, I loved to fiddle around in kitchens or tidy things up. My mother used to say she had a grand racket."

"And how is your mother? Poor Dr. Brower never did recover from the shock of losing her. He's had at least a dozen office nurses since your folks moved to Oregon. None work out to his satisfaction."

"Mom's fine. I think she misses nursing and plans to get back into it as soon as that trailer camp is squared away."

"She should, you know. Knowledge becomes obsolescent so rapidly these days. You might suggest that she take a few courses or help out in a local hospital on a part-time basis until she does come back to work. That way she'll keep her knowledge up to date."

"Once a month, every month, I brief her on new developments at Butterick, Mrs. Dolezal."

"Good."

Mrs. Dolezal sipped and thought for a minute or so, her gaze fixed on the scrap of river visible through the view window. Presently she said, "I've decided the mystery ought to be explained to you, Betty. After all, you've made an excellent record at the hospital, and excellence is entitled to some consideration."

"The transfer, Mrs. Dolezal?"

"Why do you ask?"

Betty shrugged. "The whole thing seemed odd from the beginning, frankly. Dr. Peake wanted to keep me, and under his leadership the surgical department of Butterick Hospital has made quite a name for itself. It seemed strange that the wishes of a successful department head would be totally disregarded. You're not the type to disregard a doctor's wishes."

"I see."

"Then Dr. Wynkoop wanted me in rehab. Rehab is also developing a fine reputation, and Dr. Wynkoop isn't the sort who badgers anyone with too many special requests. But his request was turned down. Along about then I decided there was a great deal going on that I knew nothing about."

"Was that when you decided to withdraw your resignation?"

"No. I withdrew it because it had been written in anger. I'd cooled off by the time I visited Miss Haskell, and she gave me a graceful way out."

"I see. Fine. The letter isn't a part of your official record, by the way. Now let's get to the mystery. I'm disappointed in Linda MacDonnell. I continue to believe she's probably the most brilliant nurse we ever trained or graduated, and I continue to believe she'll develop into one of the finest ward chiefs in our history. But something is wrong. Her performance just doesn't measure up to her potential. It can't be lack of knowledge or ability. We have a good idea of a nurse's knowledge and ability, I assure you, long before she's given a position of responsibility. Frankly, I think the trouble involves her attitude or personality or both."

"Well, that's a huge ward, Mrs. Dolezal. Seventy beds! And who are the patients? Welfare cases! And where do many of them come from? The gutter, the waterfront, the slums. I'd expect trouble in such a ward. Everything's loaded against the chief nurse."

"Hmmm, you've been doing homework, I take it."

Betty laughed. "Believe it or not, I haven't. But ever since my assignment was announced, I've been getting telephone calls from the different girls and boys who've had duty there. Right now, the condolences outnumber the congratulations ten to one."

"Well, don't be too certain, Betty, that the condition is inherent in the setup and function of Ward J. Let me tell you something in my personal experience. In World War II I was attached to a field-hospital unit to which the wounded were taken during the Battle of the Bulge. Far too many of the boys had badly frozen or frostbitten feet or legs. We did far more amputations than I care to recall. But the point is that despite field conditions, pain, limb loss, shock, and what have you, my nurses kept perfect order in the evacuation wards. In other words, these things can be done."

"I see."

"Now I'll admit something to you, Betty. You're quite right about my reluctance to disregard a doctor's wishes. But your record is excellent, you have discretion, and you don't happen to be one of those deadly female creatures who are interested upon reaching the top of the heap.

So you struck me as being the perfect person for the job I want done, and that word was passed along to Miss Haskell."

"Oh?"

"I want a full book on Linda's methods, attitudes and personnel relations. I want it every week. Also, I want a most detailed report on ward conditions and — "

"You want me to *spy* on Linda?"

"That isn't quite the word. I want you to appraise her, her work, the functioning of the ward."

"But that would be disloyal!"

"Not in the long run. Betty, let me go deeper into the mystery. Prior to Linda's short-lived marriage, I firmly believed she'd be my successor. Whatever she was given to do, she did well. And she was given everything but surgery and emergency and field work. She seemed to have a special gift for administration. Dr. Stenberg agreed she had that, and he agreed her development ought to be directed toward administration. Then she married. Then, six months later, she divorced her husband. Since then, Linda hasn't been the same person. Yet she cares, she tries, don't ever doubt that."

"Then Dr. Wynkoop should talk to her, Mrs. Dolezal. It's a matter for a psychologist."

"I have his report. I don't agree with it."

"But — "

"Betty, if you refuse, then I'm afraid Linda will be on her way out. I think you'll agree that would be tragic."

"Of course. I've never loved her, but I've always thought her a top nurse."

"Then do this, please. The material will be kept confidential. If she can be salvaged, we'll salvage her. If not, so be it. I think she deserves to be helped."

Betty stirred uneasily. "Glory," she said, "I don't know, Mrs. Dolezal. Who am I to judge Linda's work? She outbid me in student days; she became brass because she'd earned her promotions with the quality of her work. I don't see how I'm qualified to say that in this she excels or in that she's poor."

"Let me be the judge of your qualifications, Betty, I'm entirely satisfied you'll do the job I want done."

"It all seems so sneaky!"

"Perhaps. But let me tell you this much more. Ward I has been a problem ward for the past eight months. Half the staff is on the outs with the other half. Patients complain about poor or indifferent service. We've had accidents there. You know what Ward J is called now — a jinx ward or a gremlin ward. No one wants to be assigned to duty there. We've had three resignations from its staff in the past five months. Now do you know what I'd have done long before this had Linda's record not been absolutely outstanding?"

"You'd have demoted her?"

"Yes. A demotion and transfer. But how in the world can I develop a sound staff from bottom to top if I'm governed by just results alone?

She has the knowledge and she has the ability. She shouldn't be failing, but she is. Very well. I must either know why she's failing and then help her, or I must demote her and transfer her. I'd like to help. But if your juvenile squeamishness won't let you cooperate in the salvage project, then I can't help. I can't help for the simple reason I can't trust others to get the information for me. So you help or she's out."

Betty finished her coffee. She reached for the pot and poured a fresh cup. But the coffee was tasteless now. "Be a nurse and have fun," she said bitterly. "I just might marry Rolfe to get out of uniform."

"Good girl."

"I didn't say I'd spy."

"You wouldn't have your fine reputation, Betty, if you weren't the sort of person who helped when she could. Thank you very much. You won't suffer for this, I promise you."

But that, Betty decided later, was the understatement of the year. The new assignment made it manditory for her to do some quick duty on the ward practices of Butterick Hospital. She had to drive to the hospital to get a manual from the library, and as she was heading back to her car, the manual tucked under her arm, she met the new resident in general surgery on the entrance steps. Dr. Vaughan at once took her arm and led her to the morgue. "Let's do a gastrostomy," he said. "This girl Bell who replaced you turned me down."

"Now why would any red-blooded American girl object to spending Sunday in the morgue?"

The sarcasm escaped him; it always did. "The poor character has to eat, Carter," Dr. Vaughan said. "The patient, I mean."

"Dr. Caskey generally does the gastrics. If you're weak on them, I'd let him do this one."

"I'm weak on nothing. I'm the best darn surgeon in all Hardin City."

"All California, too?"

"Well, yes, come to think of it. Look, I have all the instruments here and authorization to use a cadaver. Be a good girl, please?"

Exasperated, Betty agreed. But she thought the whole business a poor reward for agreeing to help Mrs. Dolezal help Linda. Dr. Vaughan, whether he knew it or not, was definitely weak in gastrotomy. He went into the abdominal wall completely enough, but did far too much fumbling as he sought to pull up a portion of the stomach wall into the wound. Moreover, his puncture of the stomach wall was larger than it needed to be to accommodate the rubber tube around which the permanent fistua was to be created. As a consequence, he had to do too many surgical tricks as he sutured the stomach wall and abdominal wall together around the tube. When his eyes asked her how he was doing, she had to shake her head. Naturally, he scowled. To prove her point, she had to fetch X-rays and operative reports from the medical library. For the next two hours, with just a single light burning in the morgue, they went through X-rays and reports in considerable detail until Dr. Lee Vaughan was thoroughly briefed on all the techniques Dr. Caskey used. When he went into the cadaver again, he did a bangup job, even making the fistula valvular by a plastic method so that when the rubber tube wasn't in place there'd be no leakage of the stomach contents.

It was mid-afternoon when Betty returned home. She wanted to think about the deal Mr. Morden had offered, but now she had no time for that. She opened the manual to page one and began to read. She took time out to prepare tea when Ann got home, but from then until dinner at eight o'clock she concentrated on her study. To Ann, it seemed amusing. "If the reports I've heard are correct," Ann said, "Linda will keep you well posted on the practices in Ward J. They may not be regulation, but they do keep the joint in a nice uproar. Care to eat out?"

"I have to study."

"Either you cook or we eat out. I suggest we eat out. Ludmilla will buy. She loves the idea of living with us."

"Darn it — "

"Study later."

Knowing darned well she needed to, Betty did.

6

GETTING out of the elevator on the fourth floor of Butterick Hospital on Monday morning, Betty was given a long inspection and then an approving, "Hi, there!" by a young, bathrobed fellow in a wheel chair. She nodded and smiled but kept moving, having learned long ago that hospitalized young fellows could be controlled best by professional briskness. The fellow rolled himself alongside her and asked if she just happened to have a cigarette. She laughed and said, "You know better, I'm sure. This hospital's following the lead of the government hospitals. Until contrary evidence comes in, we assume smoking can lead to cancer, and we don't pass out free cigarettes."

"Hey, do you have thirty cents? Frankly, I'm sort of broke. I could sure use a pack of cigs, cancer or no cancer."

"Sorry."

He startled her. "You could be, girlie," he said. "This ain't no church, you know. A doll like you could have it real rugged if she didn't have brains enough to play it smart."

"My goodness, you sound like a boy practicing to be a gangster!"

They came to the entrance to Ward J. The young fellow cut in toward the double door and banged the left one open with the footboard of the chair. "Be my guest, girlie," he said. "You sure you got no thirty cents?"

"As a matter of fact, I have more than thirty cents."

"You gotta learn the hard way, huh?"

Betty met his gray eyes. They were cold, hard, calculating. She smiled and wagged her forefinger. "I think someone ought to remind you," she warned, "that the nurses have the edge here. Now be a good little gangster and stop pestering me."

He was cursing her softly and monotonously when she turned off in the inner hall to enter the suite of ward offices.

A pudgy second-year student was alone in the suite, doing up the charts. Betty's black stripe and gold badge brought her halfway to her feet. "Miss Carter?" she asked. "I'm Florence Baker, Miss Carter. We're all happy you're joining the staff. I don't care what anybody says, Ward J's a wonderful duty."

"Why wonderful?"

"I guess because those poor men need care. I guess because there aren't any frills here. I don't know; it just seems to me that the work here is more of a challenge."

"Rah, rah, rah, Nightingale!"

The girl smiled sheepishly. "Miss MacDonnell calls me that. I don't care. Oh, Miss MacDonnell hasn't come in yet, but you're authorized to look around. Could I show you the layout or something?"

"No, you stick to the charts. By the way, I thought the R.N. made up the charts."

Florence Baker thought that one over very, very carefully. She was no fool. Picking up her fountain pen, she said, "I must work here under close supervision, Miss Carter. If I'm told to stand on my head, I'll try to obey."

"I see."

Thoughtful, Betty went on along the short hall to the staff's entrance to Ward J. At this, the breakfast hour, the staff was very busy seeing to it that everyone got enough to eat and that those who needed help were given that help promptly. The immensity of the ward startled her, but what was even more startling was the fact that every bed was either occupied or had been used the preceding night. Standing just inside the door and doing nothing whatsoever to call attention to herself, she had a good chance to observe the techniques used by the graveyard staff to cope with seventy patients during so busy a time as meal time. Three orderlies kept on the move with the food carts and coffee pourers. Three student nurses were at work feeding the helpless. Two P.N.'s were already at work at the far end of the ward, cleaning up patients and freshening their beds. All was being done under the rather bored eye of a diminutive, white-haired R.N. who wasn't above exchanging badinage with the patients. With such a staff and such a head nurse, Betty thought, it was odd that Linda should have the most difficulty with the graveyard shift.

Or *did* Linda have trouble with this shift? Could it be that dear Linda had assigned her the graveyard shift to bury her?

A fat, middle-aged man in the bed directly opposite the door misunderstood her reason for standing there so quietly. "Brownie," he called, "don't be bashful. We just happen to be folks, that's all."

The R.N. swung around. Her

eyebrows shot up, and she came hurrying along the center aisle. "Miss Carter?" she asked. "My, am I glad to see you! I feel, Miss Carter, as a lifer in prison must feel when the door to his cell is suddenly opened and he's told to leave. I'm to move up to four-to-midnight, thanks to you."

"Grand."

"Oh, I'm Mrs. Torrance. But let me show you around and introduce you to your staff. The students come and go, as I'm sure you understand. Probably you could keep Florence Baker if you argued loud and long. Florence is that sweet creature you must've met in the office. She has a sense of mission. But the — "

Mrs. Torrance never got any further. The young fellow in the wheel chair came rolling along. "Grandma," he ordered, "knock me down to the living doll."

Mrs. Torrance said nervously, "Now, now, Mr. Arneson, that isn't the way to talk."

"Grandma, I have spoke."

Menace in the voice? Betty was sure there was. She was outraged.

Mrs. Torrance said quickly, "Miss Carter, may I present Mr. Arneson? Mr. Arneson is a big help to the head nurses. He seems to have a certain influence over the other patients."

"Influence?"

"Like when I tell them to shut up, they shut up," Mr. Arneson explains "Like if a doll needs help feeding or controlling some guy, I line up that help from the patients."

Betty smiled and said, "How interesting, Mr. Arneson. What you're saying with becoming modesty is that you've taken over Ward J. Isn't that it?"

"Bright, bright."

"Now let me discuss an emergency with you," Mrs. Torrance said forcefully. She got a grip on Betty's upper arm and walked her back into the staff suite. She closed the door and stood with her back to it, shaking her head.

"My dear Miss Carter," she said, "I do believe you're less bright than that young man thinks you are. You were on the verge of telling him off, weren't you?"

"Certainly."

"And then what?"

"Then what?"

"Miss Carter, listen to an older woman who's had this ward far too long. These are welfare cases in the main, the dregs of male society in many instance. Their standards aren't your standards, and their ways aren't your ways. They haven't gotten anywhere in life, and they're not likely to now. Well, here they are. They're fed, they're warm, they're looked after. They know it and they love it. And some of them, like that pathetic Arneson boy, are carried away by a sense of well-being and by all the service we give them. So he pretends he's a big shot. Does it matter?"

"No, of course not."

"Actually, he's a big help. I suppose

he's a bully, and I suppose he says things I'd blush to hear. But he can keep some of the wilder patients under control, and all he asks in return are cigarettes and an extra dessert now and then. What's wrong with humoring him?"

Betty could think of several things wrong with humoring him, but she had wit enough to realize this wasn't the time to debate the issue with Mrs. Torrance. She said easily, "I imagine I'll learn all these things after I've been on the job for a while, Mrs. Torrance. My, do you think you'll enjoy the four-to-midnight after all the years on this shift?"

"Well, it'll take getting used to, I suppose. I hope you understand I gave you that little lecture for your own good, Miss Carter. You're young; you obviously have a fine career before you. I'd hate to see you make mistakes because of ward inexperience."

"Nice of you, Mrs. Torrance. Candidly, I was honing for rehab, but the wheels said no."

Mrs. Torrance rolled her eyes and smiled brightly. "Don't they *always* say no? I sometimes think you can't become an executive if the word yes is part of your vocabulary!"

Linda MacDonnell came in from the short interior hall. Her uniform was immaculate, her grooming superb, her composure impressive. She took charge from the moment she said, "Ladies, good morning." Her smile and voice were quite pleasant, but in her manner was a definite awareness of her authority. "Betty," she said briskly, "tag along with us and listen. It's my custom to make a ward check before the graveyard supervisor goes off duty. I don't expect all the beds to be made up, all the patients bathed and shaved, all the window ledges dusted. I do expect, however, that a good start be made by the time I arrive, and I insist that all medications be down the hatch, all reports completed, all problem cases flagged. Understood?"

Betty said woodenly, "Yes, Miss MacDonnell."

Linda gestured, and Betty followed them back to the ward. She saw Florence Baker putting the last of the charts on the beds at the far end of the ward, the end farthest from the point at which Linda began her ward check. She noticed, too, that the R.N.s had begun their cleanups in the area where the inspection started, so that the first dozen or so patients Linda checked had already been washed and shaved for the day. Linda nodded approvingly. "I think you get the jump on all the other wards each day," she told Mrs. Torrance. "I know that Miss Lowry is always pleased with the condition of the ward when she comes on duty."

"Well, I do my best."

They came to a bed that had a red card stuck into the chart plate. Linda raised her brows. Mrs. Torrance said quickly, "Postoperative complications, primarily acute dilation of the stomach. Dr. Huebner came up around three this morning and put down the stomach tube for retention."

"Water?"

"Permitted, but not more than half a cupful each two hours until after he's checked. There was much loss of fluid by vomiting, and a salt solution was given — "

Mrs. Torrance broke off with a flush, realizing that Linda's quick violet eyes had long ago finished reading the chart note.

Toward the end of the tour, they came to some rather sloppy conditions, but the quick violet eyes seemed to miss all of them. "Fine job, as always," Linda told Mrs. Torrance. "I almost hate to shove you up to the four-to-midnight."

Smiling, always beautiful, always composed, Linda then led Betty to her tiny office in the ward suite. She closed the door and settled behind her desk. She surprised Betty by asking, "Rather ghastly, don't you think? The odd thing is that Torrance believes she does a splendid job. But what can a head nurse do with a woman bucking for retirement? Long before you and I ever dreamed of becoming nurses, Torrance was carrying the load, and right here in Butterick."

"How much authority do I actually have, Linda?"

"Miss MacDonnell, please."

"If you insist."

"I insist. We need more discipline around here; not less. But to answer your question: you do whatever you think is necessary and let me worry about the consequences. If I have no more trouble with that shift, you're guaranteed a top commendation. If you can't handle the shift, I'll chop you off."

Betty nodded. She loved the tough gleam of a fighter in those beautiful violet eyes.

"Do I have authority right now to transfer Arneson to another ward?" she asked. "I abhor the gangster type."

Linda smiled. "If you have the nerve to do it, I have the nerve to back you up. Oh, and welcome to Ward J, Miss Carter. I'm happy to have you, believe it or not."

7

LIKE any sensible head nurse with a questionable administrative stratagem in mind, Betty tried to find a doctor to hide behind. Logically, she thought of Dr. Vincent Wynkoop, the staff psychologist and head of the rehabilitation center. Having thought of Vincent, she telephoned that handsome, dashing, dapper gift to womanhood and invited herself to weep on his shoulder.

"About time you telephoned," Vincent said. "I was beginning to think I'd disappointed you."

"Vincent Wynkoop, you know perfectly well I never question your professional judgment. It would be downright impertinent."

"What about lunch on Thursday? I like your new hours. I can lunch with you much more easily than I can dine with you."

"I'd really like to discuss this gangster before Thursday."

He laughed boisterously. "Never change," he begged. "Will you promise?"

"Well, I really do want to see you just for the pleasure of seeing you. But I also have this problem, and I'm not a qualified psychologist, and you are. So . . ."

"Thursday."

Nor could he be persuaded to change his mind, there being times when he liked to demonstrate no woman could twine him around her little finger.

Somehow, Betty got through to Thursday without paying Arneson off with cigarettes but without having an open break with him, either. But early Thursday morning, Arneson gave her reason to think she couldn't stall much longer before she either came to terms with him or defied him. Arneson rang for service. Because the staff was having a coffee break in the lounge, Betty answered the call. Arneson asked if she'd ever seen the moon from the ward sun porch. Betty tried to counter by saying she'd seen too many moons with too many amorous young men. He told her to be her age, and he got into his wheel chair and headed for the sun porch. Out on the porch, he lit a cigarette. He pointed. There was a moon, thin slice though it was. "You know what?" he asked. "I've seen that over some real places, lady; real stinking places you wouldn't believe even if you saw them with your own eyes. Ain't it funny how clean and pretty the moon looks even if you eyeball it from a garbage scow?"

"You've been around, in other words."

Her crisp tone offended him. "Girlie, what's with you? I kind of got the idea you ain't in my corner. Now Grandma, she was different. I liked Grandma."

"Different nurses use different methods, Mr. Arneson. Then, too, I'm much younger than she. Perhaps because I am younger, I don't tend to be as sympathetic. I think, for instance, that you're goofing off here because you lack the courage or ability or both to make your way on the outside. Your stump really couldn't be as sensitive to pain as you suggest. You simply don't want to learn to use the artificial leg. You prefer to remain here."

"Hey!"

Deliberately, Betty reached out and patted his head. "You asked the question, Mr. Arneson. I had to answer it. A nurse worries about such things, you see, and so, of course, I really am in your corner."

"You got it all wrong, girlie."

"I'm Miss Carter, Mr. Arneson."

"Okay, okay. But you got me pegged wrong. I wasn't doing so bad outside."

"What did you do outside, Mr. Arneson?"

"Lots of things which ain't your business. Now look. We could jaw all night without getting nowhere. I had a real good deal with Grandma, and I kind of miss it."

"What was the deal?"

"A pack of cigs a day; maybe a little

extra special chow."

"And what did you do, Mr. Arneson?"

"Nothing. That's what I done — plain nothing. Grandma was happy about that."

Betty turned, feeling the chill. "I'll have to think it over," she told him. "Actually, I couldn't make any deal this week, because this is a probationary period for me."

"Well, think it over good, Miss Carter. A guy can get tired of doing nothing for nothing."

Betty did think it over en route to the office. She was trembling when she sat down behind the desk, and Florence Baker, noticing, got her a cup of coffee. "Are you having Mr. Arneson blues?" Florence asked. "Poor Mrs. Torrance had them every night."

"He's had it, Florence."

The two practical nurses came in, both middle-aged women who'd seen many patients and registered nurses come and go. Mrs. Elyot, the tall gaunt one, smiled soothingly and predicted,

"You'll relax after a while, Miss Carter. A duty like this always shocks you youngsters at first. After a while you get used to it."

"How long have you been on this shift, Mrs. Elyot?"

"Three years. But I've had Ward J ever since I came here fifteen years ago."

Betty looked at the squat, red-faced, cheery-eyed Mrs. Reilly. "And you, ma'am?"

"Oh, call me Kate, Miss Carter. I've been in Ward J for ten years."

"And you, too, have gotten used to threats and blackmail and the like?"

"Now, now, now, Miss Carter, that isn't it at all! It's just that we live and let live here. Why not?"

"Because the technique doesn't work, Mrs. Reilly. I've done some research these past few nights. It appears that despite payoffs and the like, Ward J has its problems, especially at night."

The older women exchanged glances. Mrs. Elyot ventured, "All wards have trouble at night, Miss Carter. Perhaps we have more of it than other wards, but we have twenty more patients here."

A yell came from the ward. There was a pause, then another yell. A couple of orderlies came out of the staff lounge on the run, and Mrs. Reilly got up and flicked the master light switch. Through the observation window of the little office, Betty spotted the yeller sitting up in his bed and flailing away at something in the air. But she also spotted more. Sitting up in his bed in the middle of the ward was Mr. Arneson, a little smile playing on his face. She looked at the two practical nurses. "I suppose yonder gentleman is having a nightmare?" she asked.

"Could be," Mrs. Elyot said.

Aware of their searching scrutiny, Betty looked back at the ward. The orderlies were at the bed of the yeller now, and one of them was shaking him as if to awaken him. Abruptly, the yelling stopped.

Someone cursed. One of the patients across the aisle leaped out of bed and roared for the orderlies to get their dirty hands off his buddy. Three other men got out of bed, and one snatched up a crutch and began to swing it like a club. Florence Baker went to the telephone, and the two practical nurses got up to go help the orderlies. Betty beat them into the ward, however; and just like that, as if the ruckus had been created to test her, all yelling and cursing stopped and the crutch swinger froze into immobility. Betty took the crutch away. "Back to bed, fellows," she ordered.

Arneson yelled: "You hear the girlie? Get back to bed, all of you!"

Betty went over to the bed of the man who'd begun it all by yelling. She gestured to the orderlies. "Transfer him to an observation room," she said briskly. "I'll have a doctor look him over there and determine if he should be put in a restrainer jacket."

The patient stared, bug-eyed. "Hey,"

he finally said huskily, "what's goin' on? Why'd these guys wake me up?"

"You'll be all right, sir," Betty said crooningly. "We'll keep you in observation for a week or so in a nice, quiet place where you'll be alone."

Arneson came pushing along in his wheel chair. "Miss Carter," he said, "don't get mad at old Giovanni. He gets these nightmares lots."

"I'm not at all angry, Mr. Arneson. A nurse never becomes angry with her patients. I simply think it necessary for him to be placed where he can be observed readily. Now you get back to bed. This may surprise you, but men don't look pretty all sleepy-eyed and in rumpled pajamas. Scoot!"

"Look — "

Betty swung the chair around and pushed him back to his bed. Hardly had he gotten into the bed when she confiscated his wheel chair. He got the point, she could tell by the sudden gleam in those cold, gray, calculating eyes. "Yay, bo," he said. "Yay, bo."

He was looking angry and thoughtful and scared when the ceiling lights were finally turned off . . .

Told of the testing and counter-testing, Dr. Vincent Wynkoop smiled on Thursday afternoon over his filet of sole. "I'd love to have witnessed the war," he commented. "You realize, I imagine, that if you'd indicated any uncertainty or any fear, they'd have staged a small riot for your benefit?"

"But why?"

"Why are people usually more polite to strangers than to their relatives? Why do men snap and snarl at their wives? In the case of the ward, of course, you have bored, frustrated, frightened men. Some are alcoholics who can't get drink; others are — well, nerves tighten, tempers snap, and there's an explosion."

"Arneson was at the bottom of it, Vince. I'd like to transfer him to rehab."

"Dear girl, thank you so terribly much!"

"For two reasons, Vince, believe it or not. The first is that he's young and needs a physical and psychological helping hand. The other reason is that he has the patients and most of my staff rather cowed."

He asked worriedly, "Aren't you putting your neck out, Betty? These transfer requests usually come through channels. Let me tell you about Linda MacDonnell. She's a stickler for regulations."

"I have her authority to do whatever's necessary to get the ward in shape, Vince."

"And you ask me the favor because I let you down on the other thing, eh?"

"No. I won't ever forgive you for that, Vince. It was cold-blooded, mean. You knew very well how much the rehab assignment meant to me, and you threw me to the dogs to pick up points with Dr. Peake."

"Then why should I bother to help you now?"

"Because I'll stake my badge on the

prediction that you can help Arneson and that you're probably the only doctor in town who can."

He was interested. "He's a difficult case, eh? Really difficult?"

"Well, figure it out, Vince. He's lost his left leg. He's had only a grade school education. He's been in jail more than once. He's not trained to earn a living. He's angry, he's frustrated, he's ruthless, he's mean. I'd call him one of your more challenging cases."

"By the way, I didn't throw you to the dogs. I was asked by Dr. Stenberg himself if I'd withdraw my bid for you in Dr. Peake's favor. It was planned from the beginning, my dear, beautiful girl, to put you in Ward J if you'd accept the duty. But Dr. Stenberg wished to seem to be humoring Peake. Well, a request from the director is equivalent to an order."

Betty's mouth rounded, but she said not a word.

"All right," Vince said. "I'll visit the

ward this afternoon, ask Arneson a few questions, then order his immediate transfer to rehab. Now let's discuss a more important matter. I find I'm willing to marry you. Odd, that. What do you have in your favor except beauty, charm, intelligence, ability? Still . . . "

Betty got up and marched around the little table and kissed his forehead. While nearby lunchers chuckled, she marched back around the table to her chair.

Dr. Vincent Wynkoop shook his head. "If only you had dignity," he said. "But I suppose a man can't demand everything. One should, after all, be generous."

8

THE cottage telephone rang late that same afternoon. Guessing it was Linda MacDonnell ringing her, Betty pulled the switch to kill the bell and went back to sleep. When she wakened at eight o'clock she fancied she heard Linda chatting with Ann Osgood in the kitchen across the hall. Thoughtful, Betty put on a robe, splashed cold water onto her face and went to the kitchen. It was Ludmilla Bebenin talking to Ann, however. The strapping Ludmilla swung energetically from her seat at the dinette table and went to the stove. "Food for the mouse," Ludmilla said. "Betty, I don't know what I've done to deserve living in such elegance, but meet your new roomie."

"Just coffee," Betty told her. "I'm not a Cossack who can eat a whole sheep for breakfast, you know."

Ann waved Betty to a chair. "We've made a deal," she announced. "From now on we'll cut the rent and the expenses into three shares. And guess who'll do all the cooking if you and I look after the house and grounds?"

"Not all the cooking," Betty protested. "It just so happens that I love making weekend dinners."

Ludmilla turned from the stove. "What about men?" she asked. "They're not forbidden around here, are they?"

"What we do," Ann said solemnly, "is line up at the door and kiss them as they enter. Then we spoil them outrageously to keep them coming. Betty and I always say that if one man is fine, a hundred men are better."

"I guess I know a hundred," Ludmilla bragged. "Not doctors, either. I draw the line against doctors. I see too much of them up in the surgical suite."

Ludmilla put pats of butter into the frying pan. Betty thought of saying once and for all that she'd *not* stuff before going to work. There was a glint in big Ludmilla's black eyes, however, that warned her Ludmilla meant business. Sighing, Betty swung around on the chair and looked out the window toward the river. There was still light in the early-May evening; just enough to give the trees along the shore a spectral appearance. There would be a moon. Thinking of that, Betty thought about the fellow who'd seen too many moons over too many 'real stinking places'. She awakened fully then and shot an inquiring gaze at Ann. "Anything interesting happen at the hospital today?" she asked.

"What do you call interesting? There were births and deaths, surgical successes and failures, promotions and demotions, laughter and tears."

Ludmilla laughed hoarsely. "Ward J had an interesting happening. Would you be interested in hearing about Ward J, maybe?"

"I just might be, Ludmilla. But not *four* eggs, *please*."

"You're too skinny. Men like women with meat on their bones. Ask any man!"

"I'd founder!"

Nevertheless Ludmilla served four beautifully scrambled eggs lightly sprinkled with parsley. She served superb coffee and Virginia buns, as well. "I take pride in making everything nice," Ludmilla said. "Now you eat all of that."

Betty rolled her eyes, but started to eat.

"I can't give you all the scoop on Ward J," Ludmilla said, "because just scraps of info came to me as the day moved along. I understand that Dr. Vincent Wynkoop started the uproar by paying a surprise visit to Ward J to talk to a character named Arneson. I guess he said something that either upset or scared Arneson. Anyway, Arneson punched him on the nose."

Betty put her fork down.

"The next thing that happened," Ludmilla said, "is what you'd expect

100

in Ward J. All the patients who could get out of bed and into mischief did just that. I'd sure hate to be sick in that ward, believe me. They broke a lot of things, including about ten windows."

Betty said weakly, "You're just teasing me, Ludmilla, aren't you?"

"Nope. Finally Miss MacDonnell had to get extra help to quiet the patients down. I suppose they had to use ten extra orderlies, including three or four from the psychiatric wards."

"What about Vince Wynkoop?"

"He's all right."

Betty suddenly remembered the telephone call she'd not answered. Butterflies seemed to flutter in her stomach. She pushed the food away. "I'd better get to the hospital," she said guiltily. "Better late than never."

The two girls exchanged glances. Little Ann Osgood helped herself to coffee and sat silently a few moments, her face screwed into a frown. With quite elaborate casualness she then asked, "How'd you like to return to Surgery 1, Betty? I have some scraps of information even Ludmilla doesn't have. Around three o'clock this afternoon, Linda came charging into the nurses' workroom for a powwow with Miss Ayes. She was distraught. She didn't seem to care who was present. She asked Miss Ayres outright if you'd be taken back in the event you were written off as unsatisfactory for ward duty."

Ludmilla said angrily, "Talk about a sneak! She can't handle that ward, but she won't admit that! Instead, she passed the blame onto everyone else!"

"Shush," Betty told Ludmilla. "A secretary can't possibly judge a nurse's competence."

"I can read, can't I?" Ludmilla argued. "I can notice others don't have the trouble she has, can't I? I can add two and two and get four, can't I?"

"What did Miss Ayres say?" Betty asked.

"There's a wonderful wheel, Betty,"

Ann said warmly. "The first thing Miss Ayres said was that she couldn't ever be convinced you'd be an unsatisfactory nurse wherever you worked. Then she said that Linda's foolishness would be Surgery 1's gain. Linda then snapped that Surgery 1 had its prize scrub back in the fold. When she left, I had the idea she was headed straight for Mrs. Dolezal's office."

"Has the telephone rung here since then?"

"Nope."

"Then I'll have to assume I'm still in Ward J, and I'd better get over there fast."

"Not until you've eaten," Ludmilla said stubbornly. "It's crazy to go to work on an empty stomach."

Betty did precisely that, however. It took her forty-five minutes to dress and to drive to old Butterick, and the more she thought about the startling things she'd been told the less interested she felt in eating. She entered the hospital by way of the emergency suite, hoping that possibly Rolfe might be there, as he sometimes was, and that she could wangle a few minutes alone with him. The brightly lit receiving room was empty, but the click of her Cuban heels on the terrazzo floor brought Rhoda Meyerson out to investigate. Rhoda smiled sunnily. "Why, hello there," she called. "We were just talking about you a few minutes ago."

"Pleasantly, I hope."

"Here in emergency we love everyone," Rhoda said simply. "Come on to the lounge and have coffee."

"I was looking for Rolfe."

"Not here. How do you like Ward J, and would you exchange your rank and duty there to rejoin us here?"

"You know me, Rhoda. My folks raised me to sink my teeth into a job and never let go."

"I know, dear. But sometimes it's prudent to let go and grab something else."

Rhoda sighed, looking embarrassed. Then she said, meeting Betty's eyes squarely, "You're not without friends in this suite, you know. I enjoyed having you in my crew. I admired your work, I respected your attitude. I don't know if you're aware of it, but I wrote a commendation for you before they transferred you to Surgery 1."

"I knew it."

"I don't do those things lightly, Betty. I expect any nurse here to be competent and cool in an emergency. But you brought something extra to the work — a human touch, a basic understanding of people and the needs of people in a tough spot."

"I'm sure you exaggerate, Rhoda, but thanks."

"Alright, then. I've said what I wanted to say ever since I heard Linda MacDonnell's out to chop your head off. I don't want you quitting Butterick in a huff to go work as a highly paid nurse in some doctor's office. Butterick needs you. I need you and I want you. Understood?"

Betty nodded. Touched, made more

or less speechless by emotion, she smiled faintly at Rhoda and then continued on through the receiving room to the lobby door. Empty, deeply shadowed, beautifully quiet, the lobby struck her as a proper place in which to sit and think things over. There was a time for thinking and a time for action, she decided, and this, unfortunately, was a time for action. So she ignored the comfortable chairs and couches and went to the row of elevators to the left of the reception desk and pressed the call button. She got elevator No. 3. It was being operated by a candy-striper who looked askance at a woman in a wool suit who was apparently trying to get up to the wards long after the evening visiting hours. The candy-striper was too tactful a creature, it developed, to wax tough right off. "Have you a pass, miss?" she asked. "Special visitors require passes. I'm sure the receptionist will give you one."

"I'm Betty Carter of Ward J," Betty told her. She took out her identification card. The candy-striper examined it carefully before she stepped back and let Betty enter the car. "Sorry to be squiffy," the girl said, "but a person just can't be too careful. A reporter tried to get upstairs only about an hour ago. What's going on in Ward J, Miss Carter? I've heard all sorts of rumors all evening long."

"Why would a reporter want to get upstairs?"

The girl had been too well trained, however, to volunteer any real information. She ran Betty up, and stood quietly watching until Betty turned into the Ward J entrance.

No one cheered her sudden arrival in the staff suite. Mrs. Torrance regarded her coolly in the small head nurse's office, then shifted her gaze back to the window fronting the ward. "We've had a busy afternoon," Mrs. Torrance informed her. "I think that if I ever again have such an afternoon, I'll heed my husband's wishes and retire."

Betty glanced out at the ward.

Most of the men were just lying or sitting on their beds, talking in low tones. Here and there were patients, though, who seemed to delight in the work of window repair that was still going on. "I wonder what caused the commotion?" she asked. "Is it to be in your report?"

"No. The answer should occur to you, Miss Carter, when I tell you that Arneson was transferred to rehab about an hour before the first unpleasantness began. I must say frankly to you that it's a foolish exec who takes any drastic action until she's observed a ward thoroughly and become fully acquainted with its patients, its techniques, its staff, its philosophy."

Betty took it gracefully, realizing it was fatigue and emotional reaction talking. She went on to Linda MacDonnell's office and knocked, sure that a conscientious nurse such as Linda would be standing by in the event she were again needed out in the ward.

Linda called a pleasant invitation to enter, but her smile faded when Betty stepped in. "I thought you were Torrance," she said. "Well, now that you're here, sit down and listen, please. We've had an afternoon. We owe it to you, it develops. I won't say many of the things I want to say because I'm too angry to be entirely fair. Let me simply say that you're quite unqualified for ward duty. I've informed Mrs. Dolezal, and I've requested that you be transferred. I'll take over the graveyard tonight. There; I believe that covers everything I want to say at the moment. Dismissed."

"I'd have to demand a review, Linda."

"I advise you not to. The transfer can be accomplished without embarrassment to you. Let well enough alone, Betty."

"Still, I'd demand a review. It's always convenient to blame the new girl for the inevitable consequences of poor administrative policy. I've sometimes been tempted to use that technique myself. I haven't, though. And you won't in this case."

"You're now an authority on administrative policy?"

"I think I'm an authority on one of the things that's wrong with Ward J. Officially or unofficially, you came to terms with Arneson, a long-term patient, to enforce the peace or discipline you felt unable to enforce. Now I've not been here today, but I'll bet a dime to a penny that the riot followed a demand for Arneson's return to Ward J. Right or wrong?"

"I'm too angry and too tired to debate it, Betty."

Betty stood up promptly. "All right, Linda. But I had to warn you I'd demand a review. I'm suspended, I take it?"

"A review will get you nothing! I'm the wheel here! You did unsatisfactory work, and now you're trying to cover up by threatening unpleasantness if I chop you off. Well, you go right ahead, if you want to be silly."

110

"I'll go right ahead, Linda, I promise you."

Betty got just as far as the door. There she was stopped by Linda's furious: "Why won't you take Surgery 1? It's all arranged!"

"Do I go to work tonight or don't I, Linda?"

"No."

"I'm sorry, Linda I really am."

This time Betty got out the door. Thoughtful, worried about Linda, she drove aimlessly all over Hardin City before she went home to the cottage and the river.

9

THE suspension was terminated with apologies the next morning by Mrs. Dolezal herself, and the review Betty had demanded was scheduled for June sixth. Betty saw in the latter decision an attempt by Mrs. Dolezal to let the whole thing wither on the vine. She gave Mrs. Dolezal credit for cleverness. Yet the cleverness had the effect of making things awkward for her during the next two weeks. Her practical nurses and orderlies naturally assumed she was to be replaced shortly, and this assumption made it difficult for her to establish even a fairly good working relationship with them. The staff did its duty from day to day with reasonable efficiency and dispatch, but its morale was low, and a type of "What's the use?" attitude blocked development of a top staff that could establish and maintain good control of the ward at all times.

Oddly enough, the patients themselves responded to her efforts much more satisfactorily than the staff did. The speed with which she'd dealt with Giovanni and Arneson completely and finally seemed to have given other troublemakers in the ward food for thought. During her first post-riot contact with the patients around six o'clock on Saturday morning, she noticed many speculative glances directed at her, and she also noticed a quite respectful attitude toward her. Not wanting any patient to fear her even for an instant, she took special pains to chat pleasantly with each patient. In each conversation, sooner or later, she contrived an opportunity to say lightly, "Don't think I don't love you or worry about you, mister. If I didn't care what happens to people, I wouldn't be a nurse." Over the weekend she baked several chocolate cakes, and at breakfast on Tuesday morning she distributed generous slices to all patients whose diets and physical condition allowed them the treat of home-made cake. One fellow, about fifty and somewhat cynical, asked amusedly, "Are you trying to fatten us for the kill, Miss Carter?" But most of the men saw in the cakes the thing she had really baked into them: an interest in doing anything and everything she could to make their hospital experience as agreeable and comfortable as possible. They accepted, speculated, behaved.

Linda, of course, remained impossible. In a way, the termination of the suspension by Mrs. Dolezal put Linda in an awkward position, too. While none of the Ward J staff seriously doubted Linda would triumph in the end, her failure to get rid of Betty promptly had the effect of tarnishing her reputation both as a comer in the hospital hierarchy and as a tough exec to cope with. So, logically, Linda was constrained to prove her toughness all over again. She proceeded to do exactly that with considerable imagination and misleading charm. At the end of the first week of the grace period Mrs. Dolezal had decreed, Linda paid a surprise visit to the offices at three in the morning. It so happened that Betty was busy at bed No. 29, relieving the discomfort of an integumentary case involving dermatoplasty. In this case an epitheliomatous growth on the sole of the right foot had been removed, and a pedicle graft from the other thigh had then been applied to take its place, all parts being immobilized with reinforced plaster of Paris casts for the healing period. With his legs held in an extremely uncomfortable position by the cast appliance, the more or less helpless patient was entitled, in Betty's opinion, to any and all nursing services she could possibly perform for him, and she was sponging his hot face and jollying him when one of the orderlies hurried over to tell her of Miss Linda MacDonnell's visit. Betty got to the office as soon as she decently could.

Linda arched her brows. With Mrs. Elyot and Mrs. Reilly listening, Linda said crisply, "I didn't know, Betty, that our practical nurses are incapable of seeing to the routine needs of our patients. It might be well for you to confine your efforts to supervision."

As she always did when disturbed, Betty clasped her hands behind her back and nodded woodenly.

"Supervision is an art not acquired easily," Linda went on. "One requires experience, much experience. But there are guidelines if one is willing to use them. For example, Betty, it's always well to assume others are competent to perform the work they're paid to perform."

Again, Betty just nodded.

Linda smiled faintly. "I didn't come here to lecture, of course. I like to pay surprise visits from time to time to check up on things in general. It's certainly well that I did so this morning. The workroom is in a dreadful mess. Don't you insist that it be kept in perfect order at all times?"

"No, Miss MacDonnell."

"You're honest, aren't you? May I ask why you don't insist upon perfect order in there?"

"Two cleanups a shift are enough, I find. I'd rather have my staff out here, ready to go into the ward as soon as needed."

"But should there be an emergency — "

"The dressings and emergency carts are always ready and in perfect order, Miss MacDonnell."

"Really? Do let me see! Perfect order is such a rarity around Ward J!"

The inspection, conducted on the spot, was brief but deadly. Linda first checked the dressings cart for the various solutions and ointments called for by the regulations. There was no acriflavine, no Lassar's paste, and the metaphen supply was practically exhausted. Worse, the set of dressing instruments was short one pair of plain anatomical forceps and a grooved director.

"Do you check the cart just twice a shift, too?" Linda asked sarcastically.

Betty carefully avoided looking at the senior student nurse who should have checked the carts long ago. She also carefully avoided answering the barbed question.

"I use the demerit system around here," Linda said briskly. "A rather insulting system to use with adults, but effective. I'm afraid you've picked up a demerit, Betty."

"Thanks, Miss MacDonnell."

"Don't ever be flippant, Betty. Flippancy always costs demerits, as in this case. You now have two demerits. Would you care for three?"

Just for the fun of it, Betty asked, "Isn't it forbidden, Miss MacDonnell, for a supervisor to rebuke a registered nurse in the presence of students?"

Linda's nostrils pinched together. She left without another word, not defeatedly but thoughtfully.

And that was the beginning of as difficult a two-week period as Betty had ever experienced in her life, a period made all the more difficult for her by a suspicion that Linda needed her sympathy and understanding as badly as any of the patients in Ward J. Linda never again made the error of rebuking her before the students or even the P.N.'s, but she kept the pressure on with surprise inspections, fault-findings, and stinging rebukes in the privacy of her office. Twice during that period Betty almost told her off. On each occasion, however, the violet eyes informed her that a tantrum would please Linda enormously. Linda's obvious intention was to compel either a resignation or an acceptance of a transfer, but, naturally, an actionable tantrum would suit her even better. So Betty held her tongue, much to her own surprise. At the end of the second rebuke, wondering why she ever put up with such nonsense, she went gloomily back to the ward to supervise the feeding of several totally helpless patients. She took over the feeding of a burn case, and the patient, noticing her unusual gloom, asked if she was crazy or something. Betty met his big brown eyes. "I mean," he said, "you can skin a cat lots of ways if a cat gives you a pain. You know all you have to do? Just let the right boys know you want her to look bad. They can make her look bad pretty quick."

"Really?"

"You're funny, Miss Carter. You can be tough with us but not with her. How come?"

"I didn't realize I was tough with any of you. I shouldn't be. I'm here to help, not to clobber."

"You keep a tight rein, lady."

Betty laughed. "Oh, that? But that's for your own good. We can't have turmoil here and do proper work. I realize most of you aren't in critical condition, but you can't have a proper hospital ward unless you make it one."

"The guys are on your side, I guess. A lot of us have been pushed around in our time, so we bleed for others that get pushed around."

"I can handle it."

"You've got a sad-sack blue under your eyes, lady. You don't look as full of bounce as you used to, neither."

"Let's eat breakfast, shall we? Eating shouldn't be hurried, but I don't have too much time . . ."

"Push her back, lady."

"Now, now."

"I'd do it. Every time she pushed me around, I'd push her around. She'd get the point and stop riding you. She's no dope, that doll."

"But she is my superior, you know, and you don't push superiors around."

"Boy," he marveled, "you're real gone, aren't you?"

He said nothing more, blissfully yielding himself to the pleasure of eating a fine breakfast knowing that he was scheduled for some painful dressing changes that morning, Betty treated him to a third cup of coffee before returning to her little office to make out the last of the ward night report.

The words came easily for a time, but then the advice of the burn case popped into her head and she began to wonder if she could lose anything important by taking at least some of the advice. While she was pondering that, Linda came in purposefully. "I do think," Linda said acidly, "that the more critical cases ought to have other than routine treatment, Betty. I refer specifically to bed No. 49. I found him in pain. There's no excuse for ignoring a patient in pain. I'm afraid you have another demerit."

"Really? How many so far?"

"Fourteen. Oh, I know what you're thinking. You think you'll make much of the fact that all the demerits were put into your record after Mrs. Dolezal prevented your transfer. My case is quite well documented, I assure you."

That was just too much. Betty closed the record book and said flatly. "Mine is documented, too, Linda. I know it never occurred to you that two could construct a case, but I have."

"For example?"

"At the proper time, Linda, a proper time."

Betty glanced at her wristwatch started to rise.

"All you have to do," Linda sa tensely, "is accept a transfer."

"What are you afraid of, Lind — that you'll be out and I'll replace you?"

"Ridiculous! Compare your record and mine!"

"Perhaps Mrs. Dolezal has done that, Linda. I've never had riots in an area under my control, for example. And patients under my supervision haven't fallen out of bed, haven't had fist fights. My staff hasn't been turned over two or three times through resignations and requests for transfer. I expect to bring all this out when my case is reviewed."

"How dare you insinuate I'm not appraising your work objectively?"

Betty just grinned, her intuition telling her that all of a sudden Linda's persecution of her would end.

123

10

ON Saturday afternoon, June sixth, Rolfe came to the cottage with important news. Ann, Ludmilla and Mr. Morden were setting up a croquet court on the lawn between the shingled cottage and the river, an activity that was being accompanied by good-natured opinions of an old man's croquet prowess. Rolfe stopped just long enough to appoint himself to Mr. Morden's team and then to challenge the team of Osgood and Bebenin to a championship match that very day. Ludmilla accepted the challenge, her black eyes sparkling. "Just once," Ludmilla vowed, "I'm going to get the better of a doctor!"

Smiling, Rolfe came up to the porch. The sight of Betty embroidering a green A onto a sportshirt rather disconcerted him. "Ha, ha," he said weakly, "I'm

124

R.B.H., not A.B.H."

"Mom would skin me if she saw this, Rolfe. I did better embroidery when I was fourteen. I've got to get squared away. A career's all very well, but it isn't sewing or cooking or keeping house or tending to a garden."

"The shirt couldn't be for Alice, could it?"

"Who's Alice?"

"Ha, ha," Rolfe said, sitting down. His brown eyes glared at the shirt.

"Nut," Betty said. "The shirt's for Mr. Arneson. I'm so proud of Vince Wynkoop and Arneson I could kiss them both! Arneson was here six months before I arranged that transfer to rehab. Now, a bare month after the transfer, he's on that artificial leg at least three hours a day."

"Vince is good at that. For my money, Vince is the top rehab man in California."

"Also, Rolfe, I had a chat with our welfare people last week. They've talked to the welfare people of Hardin

City, and those people have talked to a woman who owns a large block of stock in some electronics assembly company. Anyway, Mr. Arneson will be given training at electronics assembly. He'll be paid so much by the company, and the city welfare people will see to the rest."

"Say, that's good, really good."

"I promised Mr. Arneson an elegant sports shirt if and when he spent a full day on that artificial leg. Vince thinks I'll have to pay off in another month or so."

"Why's it taking so long?"

"The stump's unusually sensitive. It has to be conditioned. Meanwhile, Vince works on Mr. Arneson in other ways. I should've gotten into psychology. I do know that as soon as I can, I'll get into rehab. Rolfe, there's the field for a girl like me. Surgery was all right, but awfully mechanical, and I had so little genuine contact with the patients. And running a ward! I didn't become a nurse to be an administrator.

Over in rehab I'd really be doing the sort of personal nursing I became a nurse to do."

"Oh, that reminds me," Rolfe said. He took an envelope from a side pocket. "I happened to meet Linda near the nurses' residence," he explained, "and she asked if I'd give you this. She was preparing to drive over here. I think she was relieved she didn't have to come."

Betty folded the white sports shirt carefully and put it into her Indian sewing basket. She took the envelope and studied Linda's handwriting. "She's changed quite a bit," she told Rolfe, "did you know? Look at this handwriting. In the old days she wrote a most delicate script, each letter beautifully formed. We all used to envy her her fine hand. Now look! Stub point, very broad strokes and stabs, and almost unreadable."

"Possibly," he suggested, "she hasn't changed as much as you think. The fact is that you're older and have more experience, so you perceive more than you did as a student. It might be interesting to read her note."

Betty put it down onto her lap, laughing nervously. "I guess I'm afraid to," she confessed. "Rolfe, so much of this seems childish and dreadfully unprofessional to me. Frankly, I don't think a subordinate ought to be on the outs with her superior. And there's something radically wrong when a subordinate talks to her superior as I have on several occasions."

"Why do you?"

"Because that ward was in a mess when I reached it. The men were in control there — not all of them, but the group of long-term patients welfare's been content to leave there because there seems to be no other place for them. Arneson was the leader, not because he was brighter but because he was younger and tougher. If you ask me, the trouble in Ward J all these months is directly attributable to a welfare system that keeps these men in the ward far longer than they need hospitalization of any kind. I suppose someone discovered that if a fuss was threatened, he could wangle concessions from a nurse or an orderly who didn't want a fuss to be made a part of his or her record. After that, the deluge! Well, I spotted that the first night I was there. I eliminated a man named Giovanni and a man named Arneson. I think it bothered Linda that I was perfectly willing to risk my so-called simon-pure record in the interests of establishing a proper atmosphere in Ward J. All the rest followed, I'm afraid."

"You couldn't be wrong?"

Betty sat with pursed lips and considered the possibility. Presently her sense of fair play caused her to nod. "Probably I moved too hastily and too independently," she conceded. "That's the trouble with putting a surgical nurse into a ward. Or a scrub, that is. When you're at the operating table, you have to make quick judgments and act quickly, more or less on your own within the sphere of your responsibility. For instance, one day I came in fast on a muslin retractor during a forearm amputation because I saw there'd be inconvenience if I didn't. I suppose that ought to have been cleared with Dr. Peake, who was assisting. But it was the thing to do, there was no time for consultation, so I did it. You get into such habits in surgery. Then, when you're put into a ward, you carry on somewhat as you do in surgery, without regard for channels, face, and the like."

"In this case you were very wrong, dear. You see, Linda has a psychotic compulsion to excel."

"Vince wouldn't agree with that diagnosis, Dr. Huebner."

"Hmmmm."

"To Vince, it's really the other way around. He attributes most of the trouble in Ward J to staff resentment of Linda's glittering prospects. It's common knowledge, Vince claims, that

Linda's being groomed for upper brass staff work. Well, with the exception of myself, the other R.N.'s are older women who've done good work down through the years. Vince thinks that they feel cheated and a bit angry and that they just go along minding their own business and letting Linda make goofs that precipitate all types of crises."

"I can't believe an R.N. would do such a thing."

Betty finally got up her nerve and opened the envelope. The note she plucked from the envelope had been typed on an official memo form, and just under the heading was a code number that indicated the text had been made a part of the official record. The note was quite brief. Linda explained that it was part of her administrative technique to subject her new execs to various kinds of pressure for the purpose of impressing upon them that only high quality work was acceptable to her. Having made her point through the arbitrary and perhaps brutal awarding of demerits for this or that reason, Linda went on, she was now convinced Betty knew the type of work expected of her and would take pains to measure up at all times. Therefore, Linda concluded, she would terminate the surprise inspections and would of course cancel the demerits, it being obvious they had served their purpose.

Betty whistled softly as she handed the memo to Rolfe. "It ought to be an interesting hearing tomorrow," she said. "She's trying to cut the ground out from under me."

"No. She requested Mrs. Dolezal to forget her demand that you be transferred. Mrs. Dolezal agreed. I know she agreed, because I telephoned her before I came here. Automatically, Linda's request wipes out your demand for a review."

"Wonderful!"

Rolfe sighed. Off on the side lawn, the last wicket was being put into place, and Ludmilla was already practicing for the championship match. For a powerful woman of two hundred pounds or so, Ludmilla was surprisingly light-footed and graceful. "There's a Juno," Rolfe said abstractedly. "Beautiful physique, really. Not an ounce of unnecessary fat on her body. The last time she came to me for the annual physical checkup, I had to tell her she was in better condition than any employee I've ever examined."

"Why did you sigh?" Betty asked.

He answered grimly, "Because I'm afraid for you."

"Afraid?"

"All that Linda has in life right now, Betty, is her position as the wheel of Ward J. Her personal life went to smash. When she returned to Butterick she was both physically and psychologically beaten, and I think that if Mrs. Dolezal hadn't given her that ward Linda might have — well, no matter. What scares me for you is that you're the first rival Linda has had since her return here. And you're a rival for the one thing she has left: professional prestige and responsibility."

"I'm no such thing; If I could just talk some fellow or other into marrying me — "

"Try Vince," Rolfe said, grinning.

"I just might!"

"I'd rather see Linda fight you openly, Betty. You can handle yourself in an open fight."

"In *any* kind of fight."

But Ludmilla and Ann had waited quite long enough for croquet. Ludmilla invaded the porch and caught hold of Rolfe's left ear lobe. "With respect, sir," Ludmilla cracked, "will you come take your beating, sir?"

Amused, glad to have the subject changed, Betty caught hold of Rolfe's other ear lobe, and the two women marched him down the stoop and across the lawn to the new croquet court. Old Mr. Morden greeted his partner with a hearty thwack between the shoulder blades. "Doc," he said,

"I'm glad to see you've come for some outdoor exercise. Now don't take this female quacking too serious. Females do lots of quacking to cover up their female weaknesses. You just play your game, and I'll play mine, and I guess we'll skunk them pretty quick."

For a time, to Betty's dismay, it seemed that the men would indeed make Mr. Morden's boast good. A toss of the coin gave Ludmilla the dubious privilege of beginning the match. Ludmilla went through the first two wickets with one stroke, used the two strokes thus gained to get through the side wicket, and almost got through the center wicket. But her ball hung up on a side wire. Mr. Morden played next and got through the first three wickets and then used her ball to get through not only the center wicket but the next three wickets as well. Having made the halfway turn and come through the two wickets lined up with the halfway post, Mr. Morden waxed cocky. He bashed Ludmilla's ball to the river, obviously figuring the match was already in the sack. But he missed the side wicket on the return round.

"Shall I be sweet or mean?" Ann asked, prancing to begin her play.

"Mean," Betty said cold-bloodedly. "Strike a mean blow for the glory of females everywhere."

The little blonde struck a pert fighting pose. "Charge!" Ann whooped. "Down with Morden!"

Ann zipped through the first two wickets and the side wicket. She came through the side wicket with a long shot that carried her to Mr. Morden's ball. After she'd hit his ball she came back to the center wicket with a fine position shot. She went through the center wicket, tapped Mr. Morden's ball again, then set herself up with a nice position shot to go through the next side wicket. When Ann had zipped across court to tap Mr. Morden's ball again, Mr. Morden stopped being quite so cocky. "Son," he said to Rolfe, "this here female happens to be a pro."

Ann tapped through the two end wickets to hit the halfway stake. Then Ann did a brilliant thing. She clouted Mr. Morden's ball to the river. She followed up by whacking her own ball to the river to hit Ludmilla's. Then, using the two balls to pick up extra shots, she worked all three balls back to the court and proceeded to get Ludmilla's ball through the halfway mark. At this point Rolfe sat down and predicted, "It'll be over before I ever swing a mallet. Fine game, I must say."

An interesting thought occurred to Betty. "I guess," she said, expressing it carefully, "there's more to any game than even the favorite realizes."

"Well, just watch Linda," he warned, "that's all."

Prettily, skillfully, Ann came down the homestretch with Ludmilla's ball. Both balls were tapped out for the victory before poor Rolfe ever did get any outdoor exercise.

11

DELIBERATELY, Betty hung around on Tuesday morning to thank Linda for her memo and her retraction of the transfer demand. Knowing that the first hour and a half of Linda's morning was apt to be busy, Betty did most of her waiting in the rehab center across the great lawn from the hospital. The waiting was an interesting experience. One of the physical therapists invited her to watch a lesson in the art of walking on crutches. "Art?" Betty asked, puzzled. "I thought you just stuck crutches under your arms and walked."

"Well, there's a bit more to it than that, Miss Carter. Assume a large crowd hustling to the day's work. A girl on crutches has to cope with that crowd as well as with the footing on that particular day. All right. Assume someone jostles the girl on crutches. How does she protect herself and stay on her feet?"

"This," Betty said, rising, "I have to see."

The lesson was given in a small gymnasium. The student was perhaps nineteen, a polio victim who'd be permanently stuck with residual paralysis in both legs. She was a chunky person five feet two inches tall, a person who had retained her fighting spirit despite the illness that had left her crippled. She was brought into the gym in a wheel chair. The nurse attendant held the chair still while the girl laboriously pushed her way up to a standing position on crutches. The wheel chair was quickly rolled out of the way.

The first thing the therapist taught the girl was to stand up quite straight and to support her weight not on her shoulders but on her wrists. When the girl took the proper stance, the tops of the crutches came to an inch below her armpits and rested lightly against her sides. "Notice," the therapist told Betty, "that there's no shoulder lock now, which would be the case if her weight were on the tops of the crutches. This is important. If she's jostled, she can cushion the impact by giving an inch or so in either direction. If the impact is such as to make her fall, she can easily flip the crutches aside and land on her hands. Of course — "

The attendant broke into a brisk walk the girl on crutches never saw. The attendant bumped into the girl from behind. There was automatic give to the right crutch under the impact. The girl never went down because she had ample time to bring her right crutch around to brace herself while she recovered her balance.

The physical therapist smiled at Betty. "Art is something you do beautifully and automatically, as I define the term. You see how it works?"

Betty nodded.

Next, the nurse attendant got a pair

of crutches and acted like a person who needed them. "Today's lesson," the physical therapist said, "involves the correct way to fall. Now watch Cleo carefully. The crutches will be flipped to one side. She won't make any effort at all to fight against the fall. She'll go limp, let the fall occur, and break the shock on her hands."

The therapist gave Cleo a hard push. Cleo went down as described. The technique was demonstrated over and over again until the patient said she thought she understood. But during this lesson, the patient wasn't deliberately pushed into a fall. Rather, a mat was brought over and the patient was encouraged to throw her crutches aside and fall frontwards to land on her hands. For both the patient and the nurse it was hard, hot work. A full half-hour was spent on the project, obviously for the purpose of getting the patient accustomed to the idea that falls weren't fatal if she knew what she was doing to safeguard herself from injury.

Only when the patient and the nurse were red-faced and perspiring did the physical therapist end the lesson. Back the patient went into the wheel chair. "The pool for her after she's cooled off," the therapist told the nurse. "If you popped in with her, Cleo, to teach her to swim, I'd not remind you she swims better than you do."

The patient delighted Betty by saying in fine girl-to-girl fashion to the nurse, "All you have to do, honey, is overcome your fear of the water."

After nurse and patient had left, the therapist joined Betty on the bench alongside the wall. "Dr. Wynkoop thinks you'd be helpful to me, Miss Carter. I understand you have a lot of fellows in Ward J who should be candidates for rehab work."

"At least a dozen."

"We can't do anything for them, you understand, unless they want to be rehabilitated. Desire's the big thing, the thing that counts."

"Well, what about Arneson?"

"You helped him a good deal, Miss Carter."

"I? All I did was ease a trouble-maker out of the ward."

"Perhaps. Somehow, though, he got the impression you care what happens to him. I don't think many have cared about Arneson during his brief and tragic life."

"Oh, I see. The young, pretty, sweet girl in white has now become the object of a crush?"

"Don't sound so cynical. If an emotional attachment to a nurse can be exploited properly, hurrah for the emotional attachment."

"I can hardly become the sweetheart of Ward J."

"Natch. Dr. Wynkoop would flip if you did. But if you talk up Arneson's experience here, his success here, you might stimulate some of those other bums in Ward J."

"I'll not have my patients called bums!"

"Spoken like a good little mother.

But any man who goofs off, who hides behind an illness or a handicap, remains a bum to me regardless of how many good little nurse-mothers I offend by saying so."

Vince came in, such a fine male sight he sent tingles shooting to Betty's toes. "What about a second breakfast?" he asked. "I took the liberty of telephoning Ward J. They have about ten patients slated for surgery this morning, as you of course know, and Linda's rather busy."

Betty said sincerely, thinking of the training lesson she'd just witnessed, "Vince, I'd love it. And may I get on record as saying you're a very great man?"

He stopped short. Like every doctor she'd ever known, he dismissed his knowledge and professional accomplishments with an impatient wave of his hand. "Not great; just lucky, Betty. You must let me show you my file on the failures I've had."

"I've said it, and I'm glad."

Being Vince, he just had to take her arm and pilot her in masterful fashion back across the lawn and down to the Butterick cafeteria. A number of the night people were still at the various tables, some eating as if they doubted they'd ever eat again, others sipping coffee, still others just talking and smoking. Vince took her to a table off in a deserted corner of the room, then went back to the serving counter to pick up second breakfasts for them both. While he was busy, Betty went over in her mind the things she wanted to say to Linda MacDonnell. It was especially important, she knew, to make a strong pitch for a new beginning in their relationship. But how to do that? Particularly, how to do that when Linda was sure just to sit there icily and let her carry the conversational ball? She was still wrestling with the problem when Vince returned with a tray in each hand. She saw that he'd gotten her everything from scrambled eggs and sausage through oatmeal complete with raisins. "What," she joshed, "no beer?"

He laughed amiably and sat down. He dug into the food with gusto. "I never get up a good head of steam," he confided, "until I've had my second breakfast. If we ever marry, and marry we shall, please remember to give me two breakfasts each day."

"We won't ever marry, Vince."

His eyes twinkled.

"I hate to put things so bluntly," Betty said. "My trouble is that I know little about the subtle ways in which civilized ladies make their big points. I admire women who can hammer all their truths home without seeming to hammer at all."

"I do know about Dr. Rolfe Huebner," Vince said. "If you doubted that, you may now put doubt aside and deal with me with a clear conscience."

"I'm not sure I'll marry Rolfe, come to think of it. I have a small complaint about doctors that I'd like to get out of my system. Much too

146

often, you doctors are all-work-and-no-play people. Take Saturday as a good case in point. We were having a grand croquet tournament at the cottage. The telephone rang. Dr. Wolston wanted a trifling piece of information about one of the ulcer cases Rolfe's treating medicinally. Rolfe was en route to Butterick in less than ten minutes. He never did come back. Perforation occurred late Saturday afternoon, necessitating some heroic emergency measures."

"I like Rolfe," Vince said. "If I honestly believed you could be happy as his wife, I'd probably stop pestering you. I don't think you could. Rolfe could cheerfully spend the rest of his life right here in Butterick, rarely coming out for air, so to speak. Medicine is his life. You aren't medicine."

"Now, now, now, he's not that dedicated."

"Well, perhaps he is, perhaps not. Time will tell. Did my therapist discuss a little matter with you?"

"Yes. I'll cooperate to the fullest extent, of course. I think, though, that you ought to discuss it with Linda. I have to be careful not to seem to be bypassing her office. I did once, and look what happened."

"What happened," Vince said coldly, "is that a young man was put on the road to rehabilitation. I'm sorry if Linda MacDonnell is unhappy about the methods used, but the methods worked. I intend to raise the subject at the next staff meeting."

"Please don't do that, Vince."

"I have to, Betty. It's been my theory all along there's nothing to equal a trained nurse's observation and knowledge of a patient when you're trying to identify certain of his requirements for complete recovery. I want to see regular reports covering a nurse's knowledge of each of her cases."

"Vince, you'll have us working twenty hours a day!"

He smiled faintly as he reached

out and patted her hand. "Good," he said. "The more time you spend on important matters, the less time you'll have for nonsense involving Rolfe."

After that, they concentrated on their meal. Vince asked for a date 'one of these years', and Betty promised to 'squeeze him in' sooner or later. She went up to the ward feeling stuffed, desired, fired up with professional zeal, and a good deal happier than she'd been in a long time. She caught Linda at her desk in the private office. Linda raised her blue-black brows, but waved for Betty to be seated. Obviously trying to be nice, Linda said, "All the preoperative preparations were most satisfactory, Betty. I didn't find so much as a single hair in any of the operative fields."

"Thank Manuel for that, Miss MacDonnell. He has a fine hand with a razor."

"I wonder if you'd like to take the eight-to-four? During my chat with Mrs. Dolezal on Saturday, she mentioned she thought you might be more useful on that shift. She pointed out something I'd overlooked: that your experience with both surgery and recovery-room duties would be invaluable as the postoperative patients were brought in. There's simply no chance at all of squeezing our patients into the recovery-room areas. The paying patients have first call."

"Whatever you want, Miss MacDonnell. Oh, and may I thank you for having withdrawn that transfer request and all those demerits?"

Linda smiled. "It could be, Betty, that you've misjudged me all along. I have one approach to ward management; you have another approach. You could be right or I could be right. Since I have the responsibility, though, my methods must be used."

"Well, I wanted to thank you."

"No thanks are due me." Linda thought, and then she said with painful honesty: "Mrs. Dolezal told me I had no chance of getting you transferred, so to save face I withdrew the request."

"Linda, we don't have to battle. I'm not making a career here. I'll leave for any other duty most cheerfully, even without rank. See?"

"No one makes me look bad, Betty. If you'll remember that, we'll get along. Now you must excuse me. I'm very busy."

12

ON June fifteenth Betty had the dubious distinction of heading the eight-to-four shift when the director of Butterick Hospital strode in unannounced to conduct one of his infrequent inspections of the ward. Luckily, she was performing bedside nursing at the time, helping one of the orthopaedic surgeons renew the adhesive plaster traction of a fracture case. Dr. Stenberg was beside the bed and watching long before she realized he was present. Her surprise amused him. "I'm not a ghost, Nurse," he said. He took advantage of her busyness to wander about the ward unaccompanied. Breathing a silent prayer he'd not find anything seriously amiss, Betty bent back to her work It seemed to take forever for the orthopaedic surgeon to decide that the leg was once again under proper traction. Then, maddeningly, the surgeon pointed up at the traction apparatus and asked, "Do you know why that's called a Balkan frame?"

"Yes, sir," Betty answered.

"A lot of interesting things in medicine and surgery," he commented. "It's unfortunate that no one has ever done a book for the layman on the origin of medicinal and surgical techniques. It's an interesting field."

"I'm sure someone has done something, sir. Books are written these days on all sorts of subjects. I wonder if you could excuse me now, sir. I should accompany Dr. Stenberg."

His lips twitched into a semblance of a smile. "Afraid he'll discover things haven't changed up here?"

"Sir —"

He nodded cheerfully. "Go right ahead, Miss Carter," he told her. "And don't worry unduly. Everyone's aware things are looking up in Ward J."

Betty caught up with Dr. Stenberg

at bed No. 67. Brow wrinkled. Dr. Stenberg was studying the chart. The case, a paravertebral thoracoplasty, was in turn studying Dr. Stenberg. When Betty stopped beside the bed the patient asked huskily, "Who's the whiskers? I ain't never seen him before."

Dr. Stenberg laughed somewhat boyishly and stroked his beard fondly. "Don't you like whiskers?" he asked.

"I didn't grow this beard easily, I'll have you know."

The patient began to cough. One of the student nurses hurried over and popped an expectoration basin under the fellow's mouth and then exerted pressure upon the diseased side to aid him in the expectoration and to spare him effort and pain. A signal made by the student brought an orderly over with the portable oxygen tank and mask. Dr. Stenberg nodded. After the coughing had subsided, the student wiped the patient's mouth and smiled. With Betty supervising, she fitted the oxygen mask over the patient's nose and mouth and gave him the prescribed dosage to arrest incipient cyanosis.

Dr. Stenberg waited until the patient had been made more comfortable by inclination on the diseased side and then continued his stroll from bed to bed until he'd come to the end of the ward. He nodded. "You have a good ward here," he told Betty. "I'm not entirely sure such reliance should be placed upon the senior students, but it's difficult to staff this place properly."

"Actually," Betty told him, "nothing's done here without my supervision, sir. I'm out on the floor at all times or am on instant call in the office."

"Still . . ."

He shrugged and led the way to the staff suite.

While he was looking through the ward log, Linda came in and stared and then signaled for Betty to return to the ward. Dr. Stenberg remained in the suite for about fifteen minutes. Hardly had he left when a student came to

Betty with the message that the wheel wanted to see her yesterday.

Linda was all smiles and warm charm. "I think Dr. Stenberg received what must have been a most pleasant surprise," she announced. "Isn't it odd how even brilliant administrators sometimes make the goof of believing all the things they hear?"

"Oh, I don't think he believed everything, Miss MacDonnell. I notice there's never been talk of putting Ward J under anyone else."

"I was particularly pleased he saw the student and orderly handling the thoracoplasty, Betty. It gave me the opportunity to tell him such an arrangement is basically poor. Patients who need a lot of special care should really go into a special care unit."

"It would make the work easier, I'll say that."

"He promised to think it over. Of course, he made no commitment. The problem is finding all the qualified nurses a hospital this size needs."

"Well, perhaps next year. We have a bumper crop of graduates coming on."

"Not good, but adequate, I dare say. Oh, Dr. Stenberg did tell me something that ought to interest you. It appears that while you may be gone, you've not been forgotten in Surgery 1."

"They were always kinder there than they should've been, I'm afraid."

Linda motioned for her to take a seat. The courtesy was so unexpected that Betty couldn't help but show astonishment. Beautiful Linda MacDonnell flushed. As Betty sat down, she could all but see Linda's mood undergoing a change. Leaning forward, her eyes narrowing, Linda said, "I keep wondering why Mrs. Dolezal insisted upon transferring you to me. Here we have a truly great surgeon all but begging for your services. Yet here she keeps you despite my expressed willingness to return you to Surgery 1. It's fortunate, isn't it, that

I'm not an uneasy supervisor? I might wonder if you'd not been sent here to familiarize yourself with the ward before you replaced me."

"I'm not here to replace you. That would be a foolish move, and Mrs. Dolezal doesn't make foolish moves."

"Why are you here?"

"I believe you call it personnel development, Linda. As you yourself have pointed out to me, I'm lacking in ward experience."

"I asked, why are you here?"

"I've told you."

Linda closed her eyes and appeared to do some earnest thinking. Watching her carefully, Betty came to the conclusion that much of Linda's facial beauty was really derived from her large, clear, luminous eyes. There was no flaw in the modeling or delineation of the thin face, but it did have a cold cast you never noticed when the eyes were open. A silly question flitted across Betty's mind. Would Linda be as lovely, she wondered, if her eyes were plain blue or gray?

The eyes came open again, twinkling, warm, captivating. "I've never known you to lie," Linda reported. "You have your faults, but dishonesty isn't one of them. I think, then, that possibly we can get along. I'll make every effort to be a proper supervisor. Could we begin again?"

"I'd like that very much."

"Good. Now, then, Betty, I have major news for you. A second in command doesn't spend much time out the ward. She has an R.N. to see to ward affairs. I managed to persuade Dr. Stenberg we're entitled to an R.N. for this shift. Why don't you check with Miss Haskell and look over the availables?"

"I'd rather handle the ward duties myself."

"No one questions your nursing ability, Betty. You need administrative work."

"What about pulling Miss Lowry back to this shift again? She hated to go down to the graveyard."

"Oh, we mustn't do that! Lowry should learn how the low girl on the totem pole has to live. I've never been entirely satisfied with Lowry. I've always felt she was more interested in prestige than in work."

Betty had a sudden hunch it might be well for her to make a gesture. "Well," she proposed, following the hunch, "why don't you select a girl? You know very well you have the judgment and experience I lack."

Linda all but purred. The giveaway startled Betty, then troubled her.

"Well, if you wish," Linda said graciously. "I never object to guiding my staff. I hope you learn that as we work together."

Linda immediately picked up the handset and asked for Miss Haskell. After a long wait Miss Haskell came on the wire, and Linda told her of Dr. Stenberg's decision and invited Miss Haskell to send up a batch of personnel records. "We'll want a younger girl," she said. "I'm top-heavy with older women, you know. I'd particularly like a girl with recovery-room experience. We have a unique situation here, Miss Haskell. The patients come to us straight from the operating room. A girl with recovery-room experience would be especially helpful."

One of the student nurses knocked on the door. She poked her head in and said very huskily, "Bed No. 48 just terminated, Miss Carter. He gave the strangest little squeak, and that was it."

Betty hustled out to the ward. The student nurse, she discovered quickly, had used her head and gotten hold of an orderly first. Already the folding screens were being put around the bed. One of the medical interns came in on the double just as Betty reached the bed. The intern made the necessary checks while the student nurse chatted with a worried patient next door and the orderly went off for a guerney. The intern went from the body to the chart. "Coronary occlusion seems a reasonable diagnosis," he said. "I imagine Dr. Huebner will want a look-see."

He went off to the ward office suite to telephone Rolfe.

Bed No. 46 said to the student nurse, "Don't kid me he ain't worm bait. Kid, I seen a lot of guys croak in World War 1. I buried lots of them, too. When their jaw drops like that, they ain't nothing but worm bait."

"Even if you're right," the student said, "why broadcast the news?"

"Yup, you got to watch the morale, kid. A looie I had once told me that. Watch the morale, the looie said, and the war will look after itself."

But too much had already been said. The ward became disturbingly quiet. Betty went out to walk around smiling and jollying until Rolfe came to certify the body for removal to the morgue. She might as well have spared herself the effort. The men listened to her, but none responded.

Rolfe came in and hurried behind the folded screens. Less than five minutes later the corpse was being rolled out on the guerney. Once the body had been removed, some of the men began to talk in low tones, but most just sat or lay there looking depressed.

Linda came out and noticed the general depression. She glanced at her watch. Although she disliked interfering with ward routine, she ordered the orderlies and student nurses to distribute coffee, and then she asked if anyone wanted a cigarette. She bought a pack with her own money from the slot machine and went here and there poking cigarettes into mouths and lighting up. "You mustn't be silly," she told one and all. "A heart attack spared the poor fellow further suffering. You have to look at it that way. My goodness, I shouldn't have to say anything comforting to you I'll bet there isn't a man here who hasn't had ten times the experience Betty and I have had combined."

Male vanity being male vanity, several fellows smiled with false modesty, and a white-haired gaffer said smugly, "Oh, I've seen things, I've seen things in my time."

To Betty's amazement Linda went to the gaffer and sat on his bed and swung her legs girlishly and challenged, "For instance, what have you seen?"

"I've seen Halley's Comet. You ever seen her?"

"No!"

The man's voice filled out with emotion as he said, "You would've thought the world was ending when that there comet come. She blazed in the sky like you ain't never seen nothing but the sun blaze. Oh, I've seen things."

And male vanity being male vanity, someone farther down the ward said, "I ain't seen nothing yet to beat that earthquake I seen in Long Beach. You never seen so many bricks pop out of buildings! A lot of them buildings lost so many bricks they just had to keel over."

The office cart was trundled in, an orderly and two students pouring and serving. Linda said gaily to Betty, "Brown eyes, don't be so stand-offish. Find a cute fellow to sit with and have a mud."

Everyone laughed, including Betty. This Linda MacDonnell, she thought, had quite a heart to go with that brilliant mind. For the first time, Betty understood why Mrs. Dolezal was anxious to protect Linda's career. Whether the staff liked Linda or not, her patients, every man Jack of them, obviously liked and respected her considerably.

13

TOLD that Linda had quite a heart, Miss Ann Osgood all but flipped. Looking tired after a long day in Surgery 1, Ann slipped her shoes off the moment she got into the car. Then, gratingly, Ann said: "If I ever catch you falling for the MacDonnell line, I'll either shoot you or strangle you, I don't know which. For your information, Betty, we're in a bind in Surgery 1. Bell is a good scrub nurse insofar as knowledge is concerned. But Bell is slow and Bell doesn't anticipate and Bell drives Dr. Lee Vaughan nuts. Lee doesn't ever complain. He's always pleasant to Bell and even compliments her from time to time. But we don't have a top team up there, and Dr. Peake is ready to chew nails."

Up front, Ludmilla hit the brakes

hard. Betty braced her legs and shot her arm in front of Ann to spare the pretty little chin a banging on the top of the front seat. Ludmilla gave a quick look over her shoulder. Her face was pale. She had to make several efforts to speak before she could finally say, "I think I've killed a block cat. It came streaking from that alley."

Naturally, someone behind them honked blaringly. Betty ordered Ludmilla to stay put and got out to look under the car. The sight of a young attractive nurse kneeling in the middle of the road brought out the latent chivalry in the man who'd honked behind them. "Now, now, now, tot," he said, coming to help, "you tell me what you're looking for and I'll find it."

"A dead cat."

"Oh, is that why you stopped so suddenly? Good thing I wasn't close up."

He investigated.

No cat.

He got up laboriously and dusted

his trouser legs. "If somebody around here is joking," he announced, "I don't think the joke's very funny."

Ludmilla loosed a joyous squeal and pointed. On the right-hand sidewalk, sitting and licking, was one black cat. She looked so joyously relieved that the man nodded and smiled. "I know how you feel," he said. "I have a teen-age daughter who practically dies every time she thinks she's hit a bug."

They practically crawled the remaining seven miles home.

While Ludmilla cooked dinner, Betty went outdoors to check the various gardens. She had a pleasant fifteen minutes removing faded blossoms from the sweet william and admiring the lush bloom of the ruffled petunias. Ann, changed into something more comfortable but still looking tired, came along to resume their interrupted conversation. "About Linda," Ann snapped, becoming indignant all over again, "I think she's playing some kind of devious, nasty game with you and

Mrs. Dolezal and Dr. Peake. That's why I mentioned our problem in Surgery 1. It wasn't as irrelevant as you may have thought. If Linda was honeying up to you today, it was only because she knows Dr. Peake is putting on the pressure to get you back. Linda isn't a dope. She knows things have settled down a bit in Ward J since you went to work there."

"Now she loves me, in other words?"

"Not you," Ann said. "Never you. But she does love the peace she's enjoying."

"You could be doing her an injustice. She didn't have to come out to the ward to help quiet the fellows. It was my problem, my duty."

"And you could be giving her too much credit. She does happen to be a nurse. I'd help my worst enemy in the hospital at a time like that. You know very well that hysteria and worse can hit a big ward right after a death."

"All I'm saying is — "

A hail cut Betty short. Mr. Morden

came across the lawn, idly swinging a croquet mallet. He had business on his mind, he informed them, but he gave a wistful glance toward the croquet court when Ann had gone back to the cottage porch. "I do love croquet," he admitted. "I know my wife laughs and teases, but I do love croquet."

Betty went to the chairs under the tan oak trees. She tried to play the whole thing cool. "I haven't decided about the cottage," she told him matter-of-factly. "I've had rough duty at the hospital recently."

"I know. Doc keeps me pretty well posted about Butterick doings. You know, Miss Carter, I couldn't like Doc Huebner more if he was my own second cousin. I think he should hang out his shingle. A fellow like him could do pretty well in Hardin City, especially in the outlying rural areas like this one. But that's neither here nor there. The thing is, I could sell this place tomorrow if I had a mind to."

"Really?" Covertly, Betty tried to

study him to determine if he was or wasn't bluffing. She found his face unreadable — cheerful but unreadable.

"Naturally," Mr. Morden declared, "I don't have a mind to sell if you're interested or think you'd be interested. I like having you girls here. My wife says that's because of some of the sun duds you girls wear, but that's silly. Girls these days look like scrawny hens, you ever notice?"

"No, sir, I've never noticed that."

"Anyway, that's the business situation right now, Miss Carter."

"What did you say you wanted for this place?"

"Twenty thousand."

Betty snapped erect. "You said nine thousand!"

"I sort of thought you'd remember," he confided. "Only I said you could get it for ten, and I'd chip in a thousand if you and Doc were gonna get hitched."

Feeling sheepish, Betty looked off at the river. Now, with the summer dry period entering its third week, the river had shrunk considerably. In many places, far too many places, the river was just a ribbon of water flowing yards away from its banks. "We ought to get the dam in pretty soon," she mentioned, "if we hope to have water enough to swim in next month."

"I always put the dam in the first of July."

"Could I give you a thousand down, Mr. Morden?"

"Why not? Only that wouldn't be smart. The less you put down, the more interest you gotta pay."

"I'll pay nine thousand," Betty said, taking the plunge, "and pay fifteen hundred down."

He scowled.

Laughing, Betty reminded him, "You said I could have it for nine and that you'd take off fifteen hundred as a wedding gift if Rolfe and I married. I have witnesses."

"Why do you think I'm scowling?"

He reached out, and they shook

hands, and that was that.

Thrilled, Betty rushed back to the cottage to give the girls the news she was now their landlord. But Ann was still sizzling about the Linda MacDonnell matter. As if their conversation had never been cut short, Ann snapped from her wicker chair, "Any woman with a heart would let us have you back, Betty. And I'd watch her like a hawk, believe me."

"No."

"What do you mean, no?"

"I know what the trouble is in Ward J, Ann. It isn't what you think, not at all. Care for some big news?"

"Vince telephoned. He asked if he could come to dinner, and I said he could."

"Great!"

"Not so great, Betty. There's a little problem. About an hour ago they brought an unconscious fellow into emergency. Just another alcoholic who'd fallen and hurt himself, or so everybody thought. The fellow's name happens to be Jamie MacDonnell."

Betty groaned, "Oh, no!"

Her own big news, she decided, would just have to wait.

Vince arrived about two minutes after Ludmilla had opined the beef stew would never be tastier than it was at that particular moment. Vince had brought beer with him and insisted it be served along with the stew. He concentrated on the dinner. Only when dessert had been served and eaten did he turn to the matter that had brought him there in the first place. "Her husband, all right," Vince said wryly. "Mrs. Dolezal checked, you can be sure of that."

"Ann suggested he's an alcoholic."

"No. Diabetic."

"Ah, that's too bad, Vince."

"He was brought in in a diabetic coma, and Rolfe was given the sweat. Mrs. Dolezal thought I should give Linda the news. They're divorced, I understand."

"I thought everyone knew that."

"Well, you hear rumors, of course. But often a rumor is just a rumor. If a psychologist believed all he was told, rumor or outright falsehood or half-truth, he couldn't do his work efficiently or acceptably. I've not ever seen the divorce decree, and I doubt anyone in Butterick has. I know Mrs. Dolezal hasn't."

Betty stuck her chin out with mock determination. "Just give me time, Vince, and I'll learn to think and behave like an intelligent adult. The whole thing's dreadful. She's not living with him, that's obvious. And her behavior suggests — well, never mind. Why are you involved in what's really Rolfe's problem?"

He smiled so engagingly it was difficult even for Betty to believe he was considerably more than just a handsome fellow come to visit a girl he admired. "You'll hate me," Vince said pleasantly. "The fact is, I've been involved in Linda MacDonnell's problem for some time. Mrs. Dolezal, in my opinion, is an outstanding superintendent of nurses because each of you is a person to her as well as one of the troops to be used. It isn't like her, Betty, to allow a frailty of one kind or other to warp her judgment or turn her against this or that nurse. It occurred to her quite early in the game, really, that Ward J hadn't been a jinx or gremlin ward until after Linda was appointed its chief. When all the trouble began, she looked into the thing from a purely professional aspect. She tried to determine if the trouble were attributable to certain weaknesses in Linda's professional techniques. She couldn't find the slightest indication that Linda was incompetent in any way. Then she came to me."

A hunch made certain of Betty's muscles quiver indignantly. "Why should I hate you, Vince?"

"I suggested you be named second in command there. It was either — "

"Oh, fine! You tell me you want me, that you've bid for me. Then you stab me in the back!"

"I won't apologize," Vince said sturdily. "The day the decision was made, I had a long talk with Mrs. Dolezal and then with Linda. Two things occurred to me. The first was that Linda was out unless some decently kind and loyal person were made her second in command. The second thing that occurred to me was that her staff was sort of ganging up on Linda."

"No!"

"Betty, Mrs. Torrance and Miss Lowry were in that ward long before Linda was appointed chief. Both had done excellent work down through the years. Each had ample justification for believing she deserved the top job. But Linda got it. Worse, there were rumors Linda had an even more glittering career in store for her. So, suddenly, all sorts of things went wrong in Ward J. A patient fell out of bed. Another patient broke a dozen windows. A gang of patients ran one of the students out of the ward. There were several small riots. Notice, will you, that in all these cases, the alertness and know how and determination of the head nurse could have prevented the trouble. The general effect of the failure to prevent trouble made Linda look less brilliant, less able than she was reputed to be."

Betty said harshly, "I don't want to hear any more, Vince. You're entitled to your opinion, but I don't want to hear any more."

"The moment you got onto the scene and took control, Betty, the trouble ended. Odd that you, an inexperienced ward nurse, had no difficulty identifying the source of much of the trouble and eliminating him forthwith. Was Mrs. Torrance blind?"

"Vince — "

"When Linda heard her husband was at the hospital, she asked for a leave of absence, Betty. It was refused. So she quit. Just like that. Now you're in charge there, and a darned good nurse goes down the drain."

"But — "

"You happen to be a fine person, Betty. So I thought I'd ask you to help me save a good nurse for Butterick."

Vince sighed.

"And maybe," he said, "just maybe her sanity, too."

14

BETTY went to work early the following morning, driving her own car through a heavy land fog that reduced visibility to about five feet. She reached the hospital parking lot at six o'clock and was struck by the utter stillness all around her. Emergency was in the early-morning doldrums, the nurses half nodding in the lounge, the doctor listening to a news program in his office near the examination rooms. In the great lobby, Betty spotted a more wide awake person, the night elevator operator who also functioned as lobby porter. He was whistling softly as he mopped the terrazzo floor. It didn't seem to irritate him a bit when he had to stop his work to run her upstairs. "Oughta be a nice day," he said. "I notice that fog in the morning always gives us a real nice day."

"It'll be hot."

"It never gets too hot for me. When I retire I'm gonna live in one of them hot Asian countries like maybe Siam. I'm gonna wear shorts and shoes and nothing else."

The doors rumbled open on the third floor, and Betty followed the long hall around to the western side of the hospital. Her sudden, early arrival in the ward office suite caught her former staff by surprise. Mrs. Reilly made a little groaning sound and groped about the floor with her feet for her shoes. Mrs. Elyot made no attempt to ditch the cigarette she was smoking. "Couldn't you sleep?" she asked. "I guess we're all excited about the news."

"I wonder why."

Mrs. Elyot shrugged. "I'd guess right now that Miss Lowry and Mrs. Torrance are dreaming dreams with their eyes wide open. It's strange, Miss Carter, but I never for an instant dreamed Miss MacDonnell would call it quits. Ward J was something special to her."

Miss Lowry came in from the ward. Stocky, swarthy, seemingly possessed of boundless energy, she told Mrs. Elyot to ditch the cigarette, scooped up the Silex pot and gestured Betty into the office. Miss Lowry closed the door with a backward flip of her right leg. "You've heard the news, I take it," she said thoughtfully. "The whole place has been buzzing with it. Even the patients found out through the grapevine. They've been little angels, bless their hearts. But that isn't surprising, I suppose. There was never anything wrong in Ward J that elimination of Miss MacDonnell wouldn't cure. But sit down, sit down. I'm glad you came, Betty. I've been wanting to have a little chat with you. I know I behaved in a perfectly horrid manner when I was moved down and you were moved up. There was nothing personal in my bleats, though. I was cross with Miss MacDonnell and had to let off steam."

"No apologies necessary, Miss Lowry."

Miss Lowry sat down and poured. Her pale brown eyes flicked all about the office before they came front and center to meet Betty's gaze. "I'm glad you feel that way," Miss Lowry said. "I have a conviction that I'll be named chief of Ward J. Actually, I should've gotten the promotion at the time Miss MacDonnell got it. But that's neither here nor there. I'm more interested right now in establishing a pleasant relationship with my various execs. You and I can get along. You're good and you're amiable. Also, you have a loyalty I like. I'd have turned Miss MacDonnell in long ago if she'd treated me as she treated you. All right. Now you know how I feel about you. The primary question is: Where do we go from here?"

"Nice coffee," Betty said easily. "I think I recognize Florence Baker's touch."

Miss Lowry smiled indulgently. "That girl absolutely charms me," she confessed. "I don't think I've ever liked a student as I like her. She plans to go into geriatrics eventually. Don't ever get her started on the subject. She'll prattle your ear off."

"Quite a field, that. Certainly it's a growing field. I don't know how many millions of elderly people we'll have at the end of the next decade, but I understand the figure is fantastic."

Miss Lowry realized that Betty had no intention of committing herself on the question that had been left hanging. Miss Lowry nodded and thrust her chin out just a bit. "I can tell you where I'd like to go from here, Betty. I'd like to retain you as second in command and give you a floating shift. One night you'd work the graveyard; another day you'd work the swing; another day you'd work the eight-to-four, not as an exec of the troops but as a general supervisor."

"No."

"Why not?"

"I'd have no time for a life of

my own. I'd have grossly irregular hours. Frankly, even if you tried to establish such a shift, Mrs. Dolezal would disapprove it."

"I see. Well, you could be right. I don't fancy having all the brains on the eight-to-four, though. That's a stupid arrangement."

Betty put her coffee cup down. "Another thing," she said gently, "is that I think you're being premature. It's one thing to quit and another thing to have the resignation accepted. The information I have, Miss Lowry, is that Linda MacDonnell hasn't been abandoned by Mrs. Dolezal. I think the information is correct. For instance, I'm to be acting chief of Ward J until the thing's been resolved."

"*You're* to be acing chief?"

"So I've been told by Dr. Wynkoop. I've not had official word, though, from Mrs. Dolezal."

The pale brown eyes flashed angrily. "What foot have you been kissing?" Miss Lowry demanded to know. "Why, you've had no ward experience to speak of!"

"I'm just an ear that hears and obeys orders. I don't want the job, goodness knows. I still dream of being assigned to rehab."

"It's unfair!"

Betty said nothing, thinking it wasn't up to her to defend Mrs. Dolezal's administrative decisions. She did believe that Miss Lowry was right, though. Miss Lowry was a crackerjack nurse with a good record. Other things being equal, her very seniority in the ward should have gotten her the temporary assignment. Miss Lowry would have been less than human if she hadn't resented being passed over.

"I cheerfully give you the job," Betty told the woman. "Probably you'll get it after I've had a few words with Mrs. Dolezal. In the meantime, why don't I look over the charts and the ward report? I'm supposed to do that as Linda's assistant, and I won't have time later on."

Sullenly, Miss Lowry barked an order to one of the orderlies to pull in the charts. Betty went out to the ward to look things over, and she saw quickly that Miss Lowry had excelled even herself this night. Never had a ward looked in better order than it did then in the gray light of a foggy morning. Even the ash trays had been cleaned before they'd been set out on the stands of the smokers. Thoughtful, Betty stopped at the beds of the more critical cases — the cardiac decompensation, the metastatic carcinoma, the acute cholecystitis. Even these patients looked polished and surprisingly comfortable and happy. Returning to the office, Betty told the trailing hopeful, "You can run a ward, Miss Lowry, with the best of them. I've often wondered why there was so much trouble on the day shift. If I were Mrs. Dolezal, I'd consider you one of my top nurses."

"Because," Miss Lowry said crisply, "Miss MacDonnell hasn't the faintest notion how to handle people, be they patients or nurses, orderlies or students. She began by imposing an almost military discipline. Then, having failed with that, she swung to the other extreme. In the process she lost the respect of just about everyone associated with the ward. The staff did its work, naturally. But there's more to running a ward than doing your work, your assigned duties. I don't care whether a ward worker is a candy-striper or an R.N., there are times when that worker must use his judgment, operate as an independent and intelligent and warm-hearted human being. Miss MacDonnell never understood that, I'm afraid, so she never got from the staff those extras you must get if the ward is to be run properly."

Betty ran a forefinger lightly across her throat and arched her brows.

Miss Lowry understood the unvoiced question and gave a vigorous shake of her head "No. I'll quit any job before I cut throats. These workers are all decent folks, so I think they'd quit before they'd cut throats. In effect, however, any wheel's throat is cut when workers play it safe rather than risk a demerit or even worse discipline. I suppose there was much of that."

Betty took the chair at the desk as the orderly came in with the charts. She noticed almost at once that the charts were beautifully in order and that here and there were notes or comments Miss Lowry had obviously gotten from her workers. "I see," she said approvingly, "that your people don't object to making extra efforts for you."

"No."

For the first time Betty began to suspect Vince might have been right in some of the observations he'd made about the staff's part in the trouble in Ward J. "I wonder," she asked tactfully, "why such notes and comments couldn't have been passed on to Miss MacDonnell at once?"

"I wouldn't know. These things were

given me; I included them in the record."

Betty glanced at her watch. "Interesting," she said dryly. She got up, knowing that with the breakfast rush coming on, Miss Lowry would want a few minutes in which to refresh herself for the hard work ahead. "I'll not be back to say good morning," she said ruefully. "I'm to see Mrs. Dolezal at eight sharp. I hope you understand, Miss Lowry, that I've not sought this job and that I'll do my best to duck it. But if I can't duck it, I'll not resign."

Miss Lowry nodded coolly.

Disturbed by the things she'd found out, Betty went down to the cafeteria for breakfast. She found a number of early risers already eating, among them the burly redhead, Dr. Lee Vaughan. He spotted her and insisted she join him at table. "We did an interesting parathyroidectomy yesterday," he said gleefully. "Right now I feel as if I might make a career of being a resident in general surgery. A hospital as large as this gets a fine variety of problems."

"Butterick would love to keep you, I'm sure. I understand you're kind as well as good."

"I didn't know that."

"Jenny Bell can be a good scrub, really. It takes a while to get squared away, that's all."

"She'd do better if she studied and practiced more. I notice you were never above practice sessions with a cadaver. Listen. Techniques change from day to day. What was good enough yesterday isn't good enough today. Anyone in our profession has to work and study fifteen hours a day just to keep even. My big complaint about Bell is that she thinks this is an eight-hour-a-day job."

Mrs. Dolezal came in. She smiled and walked over and sat down. "Dr. Vaughan," she said, "I understand you're running my poor Jenny Bell ragged."

He just grunted and nodded and left.

"These dedicated men never seem

to understand," Mrs. Dolezal deplored, "the need a woman has for a few hours she may call her own. I assume Dr. Wynkoop discussed developments with you last evening?"

"Yes, ma'am."

"I begin to think, Betty, that I may have been wrong about Linda. Technically, she's brilliant. But she has no staying power. A hospital chief must have staying power."

"How's Mr. MacDonnell?"

"Dead."

Betty's lips tightened.

"More to the point," Mrs. Dolezal said, "I hope you won't refuse to take over Ward J."

"What about Miss Lowry?"

"She sulks."

Betty met Mrs. Dolezal's eyes. The eyes told her all she needed to know about the things Mrs. Dolezal did or didn't know.

"I think, then," Betty said, hating the necessity to say it, "that we ought to begin again in Ward J, have a new staff from top to bottom. In my judgment, the trouble in Ward J has been caused by two factors. The first is that Linda considered it her property. It was a substitute, I suppose, for the happy marriage she never had, the home she never had. The other factor is that she got the job others thought they ought to have, and the others sulked and gave only what they had to give. I saw that this morning when I examined the charts Miss Lowry showed me. Suddenly I learned all sorts of helpful information concerning attitudes and even secondary needs. That was too thick! Such information would have helped Linda considerably."

"Assume Linda returned. Would she thank you, I wonder, for effecting such a reorganization?"

"She'll return, ma'am."

"That remains to be seen."

"Anyway, Mrs. Dolezal, those have to be my recommendations. Naturally, all could remain as it is if Miss Lowry were given the plum."

"You drive a hard bargain, young lady."

Betty had to laugh. "Coming from you, Mrs. Dolezal, that's really comical. I huffed and puffed and conspired to get to rehab. All the time you were working on Vince to make him think you needed me here more than he needed me there."

Mrs. Dolezal smiled and shrugged. "Very well, Betty. Do I have the privilege of selecting the new Ward J staff, or do you insist upon doing it?"

"I'd never dream," Betty told her sweetly, "of insisting upon anything. I'm one of the troops. You're the commanding general."

Mrs. Dolezal nodded and then trudged off to get her breakfast.

15

BETTY waited a week before she undertook to track down the beautiful girl with the violet eyes. During that week she spent most of her waking time in Ward J, her primary objective being to whip the new staff into shape as quickly and effectively as possible. The first day, knowing that disgruntled tongues would wag, she had interviews with everyone assigned her. But knowing that the head nurses were the key figures, she had a long lunch with them, as well. All were around her own age, all had been trained at Butterick, all were bright and alert and peppy. Looking around at Clara Bates, Mary Childs and Helene Roninger, Betty quickly came to the conclusion that if she could win them over to her side, three fourths of the battle was won. So, deliberately, she raised the question of the ward's reputation for being a jinx ward. "Guys," she said, "let's dispose of the ward's reputation once and for all. There were trouble-makers there. They've been eliminated. Also, the conditions that favored the trouble-makers have been or are being eliminated."

"As for instance, Betty?" Clara Bates asked.

"As for instance, the ward isn't an extension of the municipal flophouse any more. Men who need hospitalization are brought here for necessary treatment. They're sent elsewhere to convalesce. That was a big problem. Some of the men had been in Ward J for many months after their need for hospitalization had really ended."

"How'd you contrive that?" Clara asked. "I'm interested in the problem because I've been in the women's equivalent of Ward J. Same headaches there."

"Well, I didn't contrive it, so to speak. I simply talked to the right doctors, the right people in our welfare department. Once they saw what had happened here, they took steps to return Ward J to hospital ward status."

"Lovely."

"Then, frankly," Betty said, "there was staff trouble. Dreams were dreamt, and the frustrated didn't put their shoulders to the harness. I won't go into any detail for obvious reasons, but that's been dealt with, too."

Helene Roninger asked, "How do we operate, Betty?"

"Exactly as you've been trained to operate. It's all covered in the manual on ward practices. I expect you to run your own show. I exercise general supervision until Linda MacDonnell returns. That's it."

"Fine. May I have the graveyard? I'm taking extra courses during the day."

"Yup."

Clara Bates got the eight-to-four, and Mary Childs cheerfully took the swing shift. It was all very friendly after that, but Betty didn't delude herself into thinking the girls had accepted at face value everything she'd said or promised. The test would come in the days ahead. But at least it was an excellent beginning that seemed to bode well for the future.

Throughout that first week, just playing things by ear, Betty contrived to give maximum responsibility and freedom to each of her execs. Several times that was difficult because the way of the exec involved wasn't her way at all. Once, when she was on the verge of interfering, only Rolfe prevented her from hustling out to the ward to take charge. "You're not a hot shot," he teased. "You're a personable brunette, I grant, but you're not a hot shot."

"Nevertheless!"

"It's odd, isn't it, how each person tends to think he excels? That was always one of Linda's troubles. She thought she excelled, and she felt she had to excel."

"Nevertheless!"

But the activities that had bothered

her ended out in the ward, and Clara Bates came in with her beaming P.N. in tow. "Boss girl," Clara said breezily, "buy Mrs. Gomez a cigar. Did you see her badger that shy tracheotomy into letting her give him a sponge bath?"

Mrs. Gomez said maternally, "He reminds me of my last child. He's a boy, too. Boys are very amusing, I find."

"I resent that," Rolfe announced.

Clara chuckled, clearly pleased with the way things had gone out there. "I wagged my finger at all those men and told them we'll darn well strip 'em naked if our nursing duties require it. You never saw so many blushes!"

Betty inhaled, then exhaled.

"Half of them are giving themselves their own sponge baths," Clara said. "Clever, boss girl?"

Betty's head snapped back.

"Very clever," she had to concede. "I'll buy you a cigar, too, how's that?"

With Rolfe grinning at her, Betty mentally vowed to sit tight and say nothing unless and until she saw so flagrant a goof she had to protect her patients by pulling rank.

By the end of the week, content with the progress she'd made in the ward, she turned her attention to the problem of Linda MacDonnell herself.

With Rolfe beside her and most handsome in a gabardine suit, Betty invaded the personnel department for a chat with Miss Haskell. The personnel director's shaggy brows arched over her faintly snubbed nose. "I don't recall having sent for you, Miss Carter," she said coolly. "I do hope you didn't tell my secretary anything to the contrary. She oughtn't to be innocent or naïve any longer."

"I told her, as a matter of fact, that I was letting *you* see *me*. I think the novelty of the approach sort of flummoxed her. Good! You people flummox the nurses all the time, and tit for tat always delights me."

"The promotion appears to have done you good, Miss Carter. I'm pleased. I love to see a young, educated, thoroughly trained and healthy woman step into my office as if she owned it. I'm an ardent believer in the therapeutic value of self-confidence. Good morning to you, Dr. Huebner. Won't you both sit down?"

They did. Coffee was brought in and poured. Inevitably, Miss Haskell asked if the staff sent to Ward J was the staff Betty wanted, and Betty's cheerful nod did much to eliminate the reserve from Miss Haskell's face. "Well, then," she presently asked, "what can I do for you people?"

Told, she winced, shook her head and ordered them to leave.

"It has to be," Betty said obstinately. "I'm beginning to think that you and Mrs. Dolezal and a few other bright women around here have been goofing all along. But no matter. I can't find my boss. I call: 'Here, Linda, Linda, Linda!' But no one answers. Lost, strayed, or stolen — one boss. How do I find her? Call the police? I thought of that. They'll ask questions. What do I say: that you and Mrs. Dolezal and others around here goofed in her hour of need, and her mind went snap and she fled? I could say that. I'd rather not. So, to repeat: I'm here to get Linda MacDonnell's folder from your files. I want anything and everything, nothing held back. I have to know everything about her if I'm to put myself into her shoes and go wherever she's gone."

"It's against every rule in the place!"

"Ma'am, at any and all times in my career, I'll break any and all rules to help any and all people who need my help."

"I simply couldn't humor you, Miss Carter. To a considerable degree, those records are confidential."

"Telephone Dr. Stenberg. Will you do that, please?"

"It's hardly a matter for the director to be troubled with. What do you propose to do with the records?"

"Study them, primarily. Did she or

didn't she obtain a divorce?"

"No."

Rolfe grunted.

"Another question," Betty said. "Was she or wasn't she actually beaten by her husband?"

"Six times."

Betty's throat felt parched at that point, and she had to sip more coffee. "I'll never marry," she told Rolfe. "If that's how you men behave, just forget me."

"Another question," Betty then said to Miss Haskell. "Is the MacDonnell family in Hardin City?"

"No. They left shortly after the breakup. I believe they moved to Santa Cruz, but I'd have to check."

Betty looked at Rolfe. Rolfe sighed. "I couldn't take the time to drive you," he said. "Furthermore, I think Vince is your man for the job."

"One final question, Miss Haskell: did Linda see her husband at any time after he was brought here for emergency treatment?"

"I'd have to check that, too."

"Could you check, please? I think, frankly, that any girl can be subjected to too many pressures at the same time. We all like to believe we're tough, but we're just flesh and blood; not stone. The ward thing was going poorly. I was a headache. The rest of the staff was a headache. There was this personal problem. Then along came the husband, and I think that was just too much."

"Come back in an hour," Miss Haskell suggested. "But may I ask what you propose to do in the event you find her?"

"Bring her back to Butterick, ma'am."

"No."

"Because, ma'am, anyone can have administrative trouble. And that plus the rest can hurt me just as it can hurt Linda. I wanted to see her record, frankly, because I expected you to say no, and I wanted to confound you with your own record."

"It seems to me, Miss Carter, that

you overlook an essential point. Ward J is now shaping up. Our first duty is to our patients. Much as I might want to help the poor kid, I couldn't with a good conscience return her to the ward. We had too much trouble there. We can't go through it again."

"You had trouble there for several reasons, Miss Haskell. First, you put her in an untenable position. Miss Lowry and Mrs. Torrance were entitled to a try, but you passed them over. For a good reason, I'm sure; that isn't the point. The point is that Linda could never get the extra effort an exec needs. I'm sure Miss Lowry and Mrs. Torrance never even realized they were holding back. It's just human nature for some people to react that way to disappointment. All right, then. The record says Linda was entitled to a decent chance. And the record also says you didn't give her a decent chance."

"Where's *that* record?"

"I intend to write it, given the necessity to do so."

"Why, that's blackmail!"

Betty stood up, chuckling. "Ma'am," she bragged, "I'm so proud of myself I could cheer me! See how all my enemies are confounded! A new staff for Ward J. Now find a competent wheel to take over, and I'll go off, gaily triumphant, to the place I wanted to go in the first place — rehab."

"I'd have to discuss it with Mrs. Dolezal," Miss Haskell said. "Now scoot before I lose my temper."

Betty did, hand in hand with Rolfe. "Did I ever tell you," she asked him, "that I bought the cottage?"

"Morden did. Care to earn the fifteen-hundred-dollar wedding gift?"

She met his gaze. Tenderly, squeezing his hand, she asked: "Why do you think I'm trying to get out from under Ward J? I want to concentrate on managing a home and husband, and running Ward J takes too much out of a girl."

16

THE dashing, dapper, handsome psychologist of Butterick Hospital came to the cottage early on Sunday morning with a grinning young fellow delightedly showing off his white sport shirt with a green embroidered A on the left pocket. It interested Betty to see that the eyes which had once struck her as cold and calculating were now a warm gray. She thrust out her hand. "Nice to see you, Mr. Arneson," she said. "How goes the battle of electronics assembly?"

"Pretty good. Lots of dolls there can do things with their fingers I can't do, but the boss doll says I'm shaping up."

"Grand. Well, come on in for breakfast. Vince, I've decided not to fiddle around. We know where the in-laws live, and that's where we're going. I may be wrong, but I still say Linda has a great big heart and that she went to them after her husband died. It's the sort of thing she'd do. Linda always had a strong sense of duty."

Arneson got out of the car and stood with arms akimbo, looking the property over. The two young plum trees up near the gate rather interested him, and he walked down the path to take a closer look. He walked with surprising grace for a man who'd gotten his first walking lesson only a couple of months before. Betty noticed that he still had a tendency to over flip the artificial leg, and that the toe seemed to drag as he came off the artificial foot to take the next step forward. She pointed that out to Vince. "He overcompensates," Vince said. "That happens often if the patient is basically vigorous. He'll overcome that. Technically speaking, the whole thing is beautifully adjusted to his natural stance and gait."

"You have to think of so many things over there, don't you?"

"You have to think of many things anywhere in this day and age, Betty. Rolfe's told me the news, by the way. Stop looking so nervous! I never believed I had much chance, you know. If an adult hopes, he hopes realistically, or should."

"It was Rolfe, Vince, the first time I spotted him during my senior year. I had a sore throat and was sent to him for treatment. He said to me as you might say to a wet kitten, 'There, there, there, you'll be all right'. I don't know how it is with other girls, but I enjoyed being crooned to as if I were a wet kitten."

Vince laughed softly. "I'll have to vary my technique, I see. Usually I strut like a peacock to show the young lady what she'll miss if she doesn't respond to my magic."

Arneson returned, cigarette dangling from his mouth, sandy hair plastered flat on his somewhat bulbous head. "Them trees," he reported, "could stand a pruning. I've done that in my time. Boy, what I ain't done in my time!"

"I thought you were city born, bred, and degraded," Betty said.

"What's degraded?"

"Cut down to bum size."

"Naw. It so happens I was born up Seattle way. Apples, apples, all the time apples. To stand the apples I hadda take the juice. First thing you know, I was on the road. Lady girl, I bet there ain't a railroad bridge in the West I ain't slept under. How it happens that I hit Hardin City is kind of comical. I went into one of them soup kitchens churches and such are always running. I kind of liked their chow. You know how it is? Once you find good chow, you camp right near it."

Ann came out, fetching this late-July morning in a turquoise swimsuit. Ann smiled brightly. "I love waiting for breakfast," she said. "Ludmilla threatens to leave us if someone doesn't come out pretty soon."

Ann did a lovely thing.

As Arneson started up the stoop, he wobbled a bit, and Ann grabbed his arm. Then, to spare him embarrassment, she said quickly, "A girl has to move fast around here, fellow, to get herself a hero. Are you a hero?"

Arneson blushed!

For breakfast this Sunday morning, Ludmilla had outdone herself. She served eggs smothered in mushrooms and thick gravy, thick slices of ham, diced, oven-browned potatoes, popovers and home-made blackberry jam. Ludmilla steamed around the little dining nook and kitchen to make certain no one, Arneson least of all, starved. She was indeed a Juno, Betty noticed, as Rolfe had once called her, and after she'd tasted the food she marveled that some fellow hadn't yet haltered her for the long haul through life.

Arneson was enchanted by the food, the dining nook, the view, the female faces. "A thing like this grabs you," he said bluntly. "A guy sees a thing like this and gets the idea he's missed lots."

Ann said, "That's the idea, hero. Psychologists like Dr. Wynkoop work that way. Good for them. You'd be surprised if you knew how many people never get ahead because they don't know what getting ahead means."

"What does it mean?" Arneson asked.

"Home, beauty, food, love, I suppose. Odd, but I've never really stopped to figure it all out."

But this was too heavy for Vince's tastes. "I brought Arneson here today," he told Ann, "because he says he knows something about bridge building. I cast no aspersions on anyone, least of all a colleague. I still say, however, that yonder bridge wobbles."

Ludmilla smiled at Arneson. "Man," she said, "will we ever wear you out!"

Half an hour later, with Arneson doing the dishes and the girls teasing him, Betty left with Vince for Santa Cruz.

The trip to the coast was interesting but long. When they reached Santa Cruz around three o'clock, Betty felt grubby and out of sorts. "The things I do for that ward," she grumbled. "Vince, if you refuse me this time, I think I'll scream."

"Refuse you?"

"I've outsmarted them," Betty bragged, her eyes laughing. "If Linda returns to Ward J, there's no need for me to remain there. In this age of nurse shortage, I'll have to be transferred."

"Oh, that?"

"That."

"Did it ever occur to you, Betty, that you're daft?"

"Never."

"It just occurred to me. Do you have the least notion of what you've done? You were deliberately put into a difficult position. You survived. Moreover, you had the wit and the courage to do what obviously needed to be done."

"If it was so obvious," Betty teased,

"why didn't someone else do it?"

"They didn't have the wit or courage, you see. My dear brown mouse! Surely you never believed for a moment that Mrs. Dolezal didn't know what was wrong in Ward J! I think it screamed to the world. But Linda couldn't do what had to be done. So the question became merely a question of choosing the right person to serve under Linda. Records, records, records. Miss Haskell always talks of the value of records. She's right. They're of considerable value. Say you want a girl of courage and wit. How do you locate her? You consult records. You finally spot a scrub nurse with a fine record of courage and wit under intense pressure. You stick the scrub into the ward and await results."

Betty suddenly understood what he was really saying. She shuddered. She rolled the car window down and drew in great lungsful of fresh ocean air. The air didn't help. Nothing would ever help, she decided, so she closed the car window.

"I've been manipulated, in other words, like a puppet, Vince?"

"No. A person possessed of the requisite training and character and emotional stability was put into a spot where things needed doing. I recommended it, and I'm pleased. But don't ever accuse anyone of having manipulated you. Not once did Mrs. Dolezal make a suggestion or check in any way. By the way, that should've tipped you off. It isn't usual for a superintendent of nurses to overlook checking constantly on a ward with the reputation Ward J has."

They came to Maple Road. Betty called for the right-hand turn the map indicated, and Vince made it. The road carried them through a tract that was obviously in a state of development. At the end of the road, fronting a turn-around circle, stood a large, ranch-style house with a shake roof. The house must have cost at least forty thousand, Betty decided, and she recalled how someone had once looked when she'd declared everyone had envied poor Linda for walking off with a fine catch. She had Vince park about a third of a block from the house, saw to her makeup and hair, and got out and started walking. Off to her right she had a superb view of storied Monterey Bay, but even more satisfying to her was the view of flowers in the yard beyond the MacDonnells' split-rail fence. The foundation planting had been constructed to highlight six magnificent fuchsia shrubs, each fully five feet tall and well spread. The idea of just plopping fuchsias down in a yard without a sun break or wind break seemed to her the ultimate achievement for any gardener. Busily using her eyes and enjoying all that she saw, she quite forgot to be nervous until she'd reached the bright red front door. By then it was too late for her to be nervous. The door was opened so promptly at her first ring she had a notion the woman in the doorway had seen her get out of the car down the street.

216

"Mrs. MacDonnell?" Betty asked. "I'm Betty Ruth Carter of Butterick Hospital in Hardin City. I'm looking for Miss MacDonnell."

The woman's polite smile faded. Small in height but rather fat, Mrs. MacDonnell stood thinking a moment, finally backed into the hall and asked, "Won't you come in, please? Linda's lying down. She's not been feeling well. I have the oddest feeling she's had a shock of some type, but she won't discuss it."

Betty thought rapidly as she followed Mrs. MacDonnell into a large living room charmingly furnished with over-stuffed chairs and sofas and hung with oils in baroque frames. "We've been rather busy at Butterick lately," she said by way of explanation. "The brunt of busyness falls on the ward chiefs. I imagine Linda was delighted to get to this cool and lovely city."

Mrs. MacDonnell called her husband. A big, gruff, kind-faced man, he was quick to say that any friend of Linda's was a friend of theirs. He offered a cocktail and laughed knowingly when Betty said coffee would be nice. "You nurses can't function without coffee," he joked. "Linda's told me."

It became quite clear that Linda was a special favorite and, as such, a girl to be defended to the last. "I wonder if you'd tell me what all this is about," he asked. "Something's quite wrong, I know that. A cool, level-headed, poised young woman such as Linda doesn't drive up in the middle of the night, her teeth chattering, unless something is wrong."

"I'd rather she told you, sir. All I know is that Ward J needs Linda, and I'm here to talk her into coming back."

He gestured impatiently. "It's foolish for her to work. I've been a most successful businessman, Miss Carter. Linda is all we have."

His eyes dared her to ask a question. Betty didn't, hearing steps in the hall. Rather, lifting her voice, she fibbed as sincerely as she could: "I don't think any nurse in Butterick, sir, with the exception of Mrs. Dolezal, is as indispensable as Miss MacDonnell. I know the hospital is very anxious for her to return. Ward J has a totally new staff, will be given other special considerations. But it's meaningless to reorganize a ward if the ward chief doesn't have know-how and all that."

Nothing more had to be said. Linda came in, pale but smiling, embarrassed but somewhat proud. "Well, Betty," she asked, "must you badger me forever?"

"All sorts of changes to report, Miss MacDonnell. Also, Mrs. Dolezal would love to have you back yesterday."

"But — "

"I'm told to say, Miss MacDonnell, that the staff's resentment of a brilliant nurse is understood, and that difficulties caused by that resentment are never blamed on the nurse who's resented."

"What could I do, Betty? I couldn't fire them all."

"Mrs. Dolezal's handled it well, Miss

MacDonnell. I get the blame for having them all transferred while you were away. And don't feel sorry for me. I'm not vulnerable. I marry my beloved medic, next year I have a baby or ten, and the badge and the stripe are put into mothballs forever."

"You know about — John Smith?"

Betty looked at Mr. and Mrs. MacDonnell. She thought it didn't matter, really, if she had to do one more unpleasant thing for Linda MacDonnell. Help was help, whether you gave it to a patient in a bed or a poor troubled creature such as Linda.

"I'm sorry to have to tell you," Betty said firmly, "that your son died at Butterick Hospital a bit more than a week ago."

There wasn't a sound.

"It's sometimes possible that erratic behavior is caused by a diabetic condition," Betty went on. "I think that was the case here."

She got up and nodded and went to

the hall. "Dr. Wynkoop and I will wait in the car," she told Linda. "I hope you'll come back."

Linda nodded. That was all, but it was enough.

17

MRS. DOLEZAL stalled and Miss Haskell objected, but Linda MacDonnell was finally returned to the big job in Ward J on the first of September. On the second of September Betty declared herself a surplus commodity and made a pitch to Linda for an immediate transfer to rehab. Linda shook her head. "I'm deaf," she reported. "Anyway, I'd like one familiar face around."

"Look, Miss MacDonnell — "

"Call me Linda."

"Linda, I'm determined to get to rehab. Now be a sweet creature and spare me a lot of huffing and puffing."

"How'd you like to go up to staff?"

"Staff?"

"You know how Mrs. Dolezal is. She likes to recruit potent talent for her staff. I have a memo around here in which she asks if I think you'll do for appointment to her staff. I told her I think you'll do."

"You didn't. You wouldn't. Ha, ha, ha, such a comic character."

Linda got up and closed the door. Through the observation window they could see Clara Bates and her crew moving around with the ten o'clock fruit juice or apples. It was interesting to see Clara Bates in action. Sassy always, but always observing and thinking, too, Clara tarried at each bed to chat with the patient or rearrange the covers. No one was overlooked, but no one.

"Just for the record," Linda said diffidently, "I was badly shaken by the way my marriage turned out. Coming here was like coming home, you know? Frankly, I didn't feel I could risk doing the things that had to be done to whip the ward into shape. I just couldn't risk losing this place. It was all I had."

"Never let Mrs. Dolezal or Miss Haskell forget they goofed, Linda. If anyone was the trouble in Ward J, they were. They passed over Torrance and Lowry for two reasons: age and lack of special ability. That's dynamite. When you pass over an eligible, you must fire him or transfer him. Unconsciously, and that was true here, they'll resent and drag their feet every time."

"You move fast, you know."

"That's how we're trained in Surgery 1. Think fast, move fast."

"I wonder if I'm worth all the trouble I caused, Betty? I like to think so, but I don't know. I'm beginning to appreciate the ability you hide under that charming smile and don't-care-a-hoot attitude. Seriously, I can't think of anyone better qualified to go to staff. There's work that takes courage, wit, perception — the whole ball of wax."

"Wedding bells, tra la."

"I'd like to advise you."

"Certainly."

"I'm not bitter, you understand. I chose the wrong man. He was gay, he was handsome, all the rest. I didn't know until after our marriage that he was estranged from his family. The money he'd been spending so cheerfully on me was money he'd stolen from the family business. You aren't supposed to speak ill of the dead, so I won't. Things happened, I couldn't endure it any longer, I returned here. But the point I'm making is this, Betty: Rolfe's a fine man, a fine doctor. But let him be a doctor. I mean, don't just rush off and quit and have babies and put him under pressure to earn bigger and better money. It'll all come in time, so don't hurry things."

"Your husband was under pressure?"

"Well, I'd quit, and the money ran out, and the pretense had to end. His way of breaking the news to me was to come home drunk and beat me up and then brag how he'd fooled me."

"But you're not bitter."

Linda drew a deep breath, and blushed.

"Actually," Betty said, "I intend to be as sensible as I can, Linda. We'll both continue with our work at old

Butterick. About three years more for him, I think. But naturally I don't want a career here. Staff would be a career."

The telephone rang.

Linda listened and said she'd do that little thing and pronged the handset. "Mrs. Dolezal requests your presence," she said most formally. "If I must lose you now, I must. But I hope you understand, Betty, that you always have a home in Ward J."

"With all those fellows? Scandal!"

Linda was laughing when Betty left, and her laughter somehow made all the effort and worry over the summer worth-while. Cross off a problem gal, Betty thought. On to bigger and better challenges!

Mrs. Dolezal greeted her stiffly and gestured her to a chair. "Young lady," she said, "it appears you believe you're entitled to special consideration because of a small service you rendered this office. I'm astonished. I thought all our graduates understood we give no one special consideration for any reason."

Betty asked warily, "Where do you plan to send me next, Mrs. Dolezal?"

"I might take you into my office. I'm not sure. Much would depend upon your long-range plans."

"Marriage."

"Soon?"

"Probably in November. Rolfe likes to vacation in November. His folks live in upper New York State, and he enjoys having an old-fashioned Thanksgiving Dinner with them. I think the snow's an attraction, too."

"He could hang out his shingle in Hardin City, you know. He's a most competent physician and is well liked. While it isn't hospital policy to recommend a physician, his friends here would see to it that he doesn't starve."

"Is he the general-practice type, Mrs. Dolezal?"

"I'd say no. I'm not a judge of such matters, you understand, but my first thought is no. He's the type who wouldn't count costs, and even a doctor must do that if he hopes to earn a proper living for his family. I would say, speaking generally, that he's the type for a major hospital position. I'd like to see him head our medical office."

"He'd like that, I'm sure."

"Dr. Baines is due to retire in four more years, Betty. Logically, the position would go to Dr. Huebner."

"I'd certainly love to remain in Hardin City, Mrs. Dolezal. I've bought that cottage. That's how much I love Hardin City."

"But marriage is definitely planned?"

Betty had to laugh. "He doesn't have a chance of getting away from me. It's odd how you go along from day to day, thinking that next year or the year after you'll marry. Then something happens, and you realize you're a fool not to take your happiness the moment it's sensible to do so. I think the terminal in Ward J made me realize that. Linda was so good about getting out into the ward and nipping incipient gloom and even hysteria in the bud. But a man makes an odd squeak and is gone. And say there was a woman who loved . . . you see?"

"I've always seen," Mrs. Dolezal said dryly. "Why do you suppose I married when I was younger than you? And had there been children . . . well, no matter. Now you've given me a difficult task. Had your long-range plans included a full-time career in nursing, I'd have popped you onto my staff for development in the administrative area."

"Rehab, please."

"My dear girl, what on earth do you think you've been engaged in since I pulled you from Surgery 1? We now have a rehabilitated Ward J. We now have a rehabilitated ward chief."

"But — "

"Rehab is rehab, Betty. Now, then, we have another little problem. Next to you, Bell is the best scrub I can give Surgery 1. I don't know what's wrong with Bell. I think you ought to find out and correct it, whatever it happens to be."

"Mrs. Dolezal!"

"In the meantime, of course, you'd be making points for me with Dr. Peake. You might even say you're rehabilitating me. Could you begin tomorrow?"

"Ma'am . . ."

"A man who takes a licking well, dear, really ought to be given time to lick his wounds. It may well be that you'll end up in the rehab center one of these days, but now's not the time. There. You take the rest of the day off. Oh, and burn this ridiculous request for rehab duty, will you?"

"I'd just love to know what I've ever done to deserve such treatment. I'd just love to know."

Mrs. Dolezal laughed. Then, sobering, she said thoughtfully, "You could be a great administrator, dear, believe me. You have the courage to take risks, the wit to hedge your position, the intelligence to establish an objective and then plan its achievement. There, I think that answers your question."

Scowling, Betty left. She went straight upstairs to Surgery 1. Entering Miss Ayres' office, she found Ann and Miss Ayres having coffee and pastry while they discussed an incarcerated hernia Dr. Lee Vaughan had apparently done that morning. Little Ann got up with considerable verve and filled a mug with coffee. "Like old times," she said. "Let's shoot Dolezal and pray the next high muck-a-muck will be kinder than Dolezal's been."

Betty looked at Miss Ayres, a rather smug Miss Ayres. "I'm back again," she reported. "I don't know how you did it, but I'm back again."

Ann squealed. "Love that Dolezal!"

"These things happen," Miss Ayres told Betty. "One must bear up and all that. We have some interesting things scheduled for this afternoon. Think you'd like to get to work at once?"

"I have official permission to take

the rest of the day off."

"We spoil you girls," Miss Ayres kidded. "I think that's because we have such great big hearts."

Some day, Betty thought ... some day ...

After the coffee she telephoned Rolfe. He said it was a strange thing, but he'd just been given the rest of the day off, too. He trailed along after her car back to the cottage. But, oddly, he was content just to take a seat on the bench overlooking the river and the rustic bridge. "Next time," he said, "let's try a moon bridge."

Betty smiled as she sat beside him. "All right when little boys want to play, a wise woman lets them play. I have a better idea, however."

"Such as?"

"Mr. Morden thinks that a certain doc he knows and himself could fix up a pretty fair apartment over the garage. He thinks that if we did that, we'd keep Ann and Ludmilla around after we married."

"Well . . . "

"The income would be nice, Rolfe, but even nicer would be their company. I'm terribly fond of Ann. I always wanted a sis, and Ann's it."

"Consider it done."

"My, such a *beautiful* apartment!"

He smiled fatuously, did Dr. Rolfe Huebner. Then, as men have been doing from time immemorial, Rolfe looped an arm around his girl's waist and kissed her.

"I wonder why?" Betty asked.

"Nothing better to do."

"Nut."

"All right," Rolfe said; "let's go take a whack at the garage."

But it was so perfect, Betty thought, right there by the river . . . so quiet, so beautiful, so perfect . . .